Praise for Ghosters . . .

"A creaky old house, ghost sightings, and the forbidden third floor will engage young readers all the way through to the unexpected ending. An exciting debut novel full of mystery and humor. Diana Corbitt is a terrific writer. "
—Carrie Bedford, author of the Kate Benedict paranormal mystery series

"Be prepared for a wild ride as Theresa, Kerry and Joey explore their new home, a rundown Victorian mansion. Get ready for what they find when they get up the nerve to go into the basement. And hang onto your seat when they venture upstairs and through the door Theresa's Dad forbade her to go through. Ghosters is great fun. It is well paced with wonderful quirky characters that readers will love."—J.P. Shaw, author of *Drazil House*

Chase,

Hope you like getting scared!

Diana Corbitt

GHOSTERS

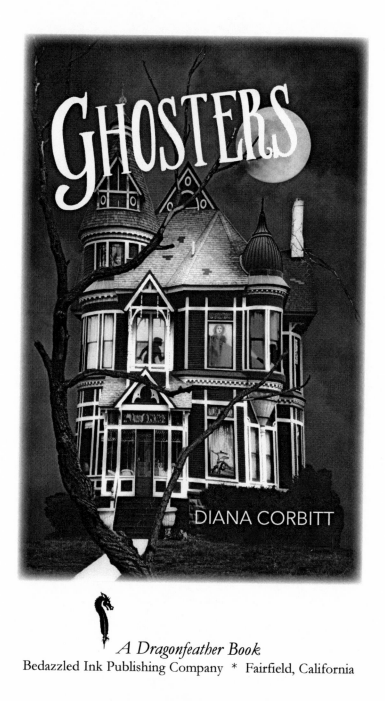

GHOSTERS

DIANA CORBITT

A Dragonfeather Book
Bedazzled Ink Publishing Company * Fairfield, California

978-1-943837-95-3 paperback
978-1-943837-96-0 epub
978-1-943837-97-7 mobi

Cover Design
by

DESIGNS

Dragonfeather Books
a division of
Bedazzled Ink Publishing Company
Fairfield, California
http://www.bedazzledink.com

This book is dedicated to all of the people I love and appreciate: my husband Michael, my sons, Tyson and Sean, and all my dear friends, especially Theresa and Kerry and the members of my writing group, without whom I would have no need to write this.

CHAPTER 1

LIFE IS WEIRD. When my mom died six months ago, I didn't even know what my grandparents looked like. Now, I'm getting ready to bake cookies in their hundred-something-year-old mansion with their photos looking down on me in almost every room.

Like the rest of the house, my grandmother's kitchen is huge, twice as big as our old one. Because Mom never bothered to clean the place out after Grandma died, the cabinets are still stocked with all kinds of bowls, spoons, and pans. Obviously, Grandma Carmen was majorly into cooking, a lot like Mom who ran her own catering business back in Crescent City.

Ever since I found Grandma Carmen's *rosquillos* recipe in one of the drawers yesterday, I've been dying to try it. So what if they're Christmas cookies, and this is only September?

I gather my supplies. Mom taught me to be super clean when I cook, so I squeeze my thick and annoyingly curly brown hair into a Scrunchy and wash my hands. All set except for one thing. I can't find the powdered sugar, and we just bought it this morning.

It's supposed to be in the walk-in pantry. There's no light, so I leave the door open. Standing in the center, I turn in slow circles and check all the shelves for the second time. Dad threw out all of Grandma's old cans and boxes, so everything in here is new. Since Joey and I have both inherited Dad's huge sweet tooth, we're all stocked up on baking powder, flour, everything I need to keep us supplied with cakes and cookies. Besides the baking stuff, the shelves now hold rice, noodles, a case of Pepsi, a family-sized bag of Nacho Cheese Doritos, and three kinds of cereal, among other things. When I realize I only know this because I recognize their colors and shapes, I take off my glasses and use my shirt to clean them. Amazing. I was blind, but now I see.

Fuzzy vision magically cured, I move everything around looking for the powdered sugar. No luck.

After snagging a handful of Doritos, I step back into the kitchen to do another search, this time with clear lenses. Five minutes later, I still haven't found the sugar.

There's a staircase in the corner. Unlike the main stairs, which is all hand-carved wood, this one is plain since it was only for servants, a luxury I can't imagine. Joey, my nine-year-old brother, trots down the steps as I'm about to check the pantry for the fifth time.

"Theresa, you said you were going to bake *rosquillos.*"

"I *am* going to bake *rosquillos.*"

"When?" His eyes fix on the teapot-shaped clock on the wall above the stove. "You said that seventeen minutes and twenty-three seconds ago."

I've laid out some utensils on Grandma's old butcher-block table. Joey saunters over and eyes the empty bowl. "Have you been eating Doritos this whole time?"

"What? No." I lick my lips, and the taste of nacho dust comes back. Geez, does he see everything? "Look, I didn't come in here to stuff my face. I haven't made the cookies yet because I can't find the powdered sugar."

"Are your lenses clean?"

He reaches for my glasses, but I brush aside his hand before he can snatch them. Since people with Asperger's aren't always good at reading expressions, I put on an angry face and point at it. "See this look?" I push my eyebrows together for dramatic effect.

"Yes."

"What's it mean?"

"You're annoyed."

I nod hard. "Grabbing someone's glasses is rude." How

do you say rude in Spanish? When I can't come up with it, I settle for very bad, or *Muy malo.*

Once he's got the idea, I drop the act and hold out my newly wiped specs so he can see them.

"At first I didn't realize they *were* smudgy, but . . ." My words trail off as he strolls across the kitchen, opens the ancient avocado-green refrigerator, and pulls out a jar. The kid's not even listening.

Well, I can be annoying too. "Did you open up all the windows like Dad told you?"

He fishes out a huge dill pickle, his favorite food. "Not yet. I haven't finished watching the DVD on poisonous spiders."

Just as I suspected. "Weren't you the one complaining about the moldy smell? If you want it to go away, you're gonna have to open this place up."

"I will."

"Do it while it's still warm out. Dad likes it when he doesn't have to tell you twice."

"I'll do it after I watch the part about brown recluse spiders."

I cross my arms like Mom used to.

"But it's my favorite part."

"You've seen that a hundred times, Jojo. Do it now."

"Oh, all right." He takes a huge bite and mumbles, "Let me know when the *rosquillos* are ready," through a mouthful of pickle. With that, he trots back up the stairs. Across the room, the pickle jar sits open on the counter. Big help he is.

I put Joey's pickles away and head back into the pantry.

Uggghhhh . . . what color is that stupid powdered sugar box? Red? Blue?

There's a case of bottled water on the top shelf, an easy reach for Dad but not for somebody who's barely five feet tall. Lucky for me, the shelves are sturdy. I climb onto the lowest and shove the bottled water aside to check behind. Nothing.

Creeeeaaak. Thump.

The noise comes from the kitchen, so I step out of the pantry. "Thanks for coming back, Jojo. Maybe *you* can find the . . ." Nobody's there. Not Joey. Not Dad. Just me and the blue-and-white box lying on the white tiled counter across the room.

Above it, the cupboard door slowly swings shut with the same eerie creaking sound that drew me out there. *What the heck?*

Ignoring the goose bumps that have popped up on my arms, I creep over and turn the box face up. Yup, it's the powdered sugar, all right. I yank open the cupboard door. Coffee cups.

A ghostly cold finger seems to press against the base of my spine, and I shiver as I remember what happened at the grocery store this morning.

"So it was *you* and your kids that moved into the old Ramos House?" The old poofy haired cashier looked at Dad as if he just tore open one of our cereal boxes and poured Fruit Loops over his head. "But that place has been haunted ever since—you *do* know it's haunted . . . *don't* you?"

Later, in the car, we chuckled at the old woman's wacky stories. But now . . .

So what if some old grocery store lady thinks this house is full of ghosts? That doesn't mean there's one messing with me right now. Yeah? Well then, who put that box up there? Dad? Me? Obviously not Joey. He'd rather eat dirt than put something in the wrong place. And how come I didn't see it the first ten times I looked?

Another thump.

Now the powdered sugar is on the floor.

"Whoa!" I jump back as if expecting the tiny cardboard box to sprout feet and run up my leg. "Grandma Carmen . . . ?" If she's really here, then where is she? Floating on the ceiling? Behind me? Suddenly paranoid, I look everywhere.

"Theresa . . . ?"

Even though I recognize Dad's voice, I spin around, half expecting my grandmother to be standing behind him, rubber spatula in hand.

He squints at me like I'm some weird zoo animal. "What's wrong? *¿Qué te pasa?*"

An invisible hand squeezes my chest, and I realize I've been holding my breath this whole time. Knowing Dad will laugh if I tell him what I'm really thinking, I fumble to come up with something he *will* believe.

"Did you feel anything weird a minute ago? You know . . . like tremors?" A reasonable question since we live in California.

"What, you think you felt an earthquake?" He runs his fingers through his tweaked out hair, shrugs, then spots the box on the floor. "What's that doing there?"

For gosh sake, don't tell him it jumped off the counter. I pick it up. "I found some of Grandma's cookie recipes. Decided to make us some *rosquillos*. When the tremor happened I got scared, so I . . ."

"*Rosquillos*, huh? Your mom only made those at Christmas." He heads for the fridge, then turns back, the corners of his mouth curved upward.

He's smiling. Must be the cookies. I bounce on my toes, happy I decided to bake them.

But instead of thanking me, he says, "Hey, remember, at breakfast, when I told Joey to open up the windows? He's doing it now, and I never even had to remind him. Great kid, huh?"

"Yup . . . great kid." I put down the box and stand there, nodding and smiling, as Dad grabs himself a can of Pepsi. Why am I the only one who wears glasses in this family? He's the one who's half blind.

Once my oblivious father leaves, I slump against the counter, studying the powdered sugar. Did I stick you in the cupboard and just don't remember doing it? Dad always says the simplest answer is usually the right one. Okay, so that explains how you ended up with the coffee cups, but what made you fall . . . twice?

I give the box a few pokes with my finger. When it doesn't do any more tricks, I carry it over to the table and set it alongside the other ingredients. A half hour later, the smell of Christmas cookies fills the kitchen. Time to update Joey.

This is a big day for the Martinez family. After suffering the tortures of no TV or Internet for nearly a week, we're finally getting hooked up. I know the guy started with the living room TV, so I head there first. As I expect, Joey's flopped on the sofa, watching cartoons. But that's not why I smile. From what I can tell, every window in the house is wide open.

"Good job with the windows, little brother."

Because I haven't asked a question, Joey says nothing and continues to stare at the big-screen TV, one of the few things Dad didn't sell before the move.

I drop into the empty space on the end of the sofa, careful not to touch him. "When somebody says something nice, you're supposed to say thank you."

"Thank you."

"And the *rosquillos* will be ready in about ten more minutes." Joey's lack of eye contact is something we've been working on, so I tap his foot with my finger.

He looks at me between blinks. "Thank you. And there's white stuff on your left lens."

I yank my glasses off and hold them up to the light. Geez, he's right. Flour.

As I'm cleaning them, we hear Dad and the cable guy make their way down the main staircase to the foyer. After handshakes and goodbyes, Dad strides over to us.

"We're set. All the TVs and computers are officially operational."

"Is this another thank you situation?" Joey asks, eyes never leaving the TV.

"Yes." I stand up. "Thanks, Dad. That's great. And I made the *rosquillos*. They'll be ready in about—"

Dad steps past me and smiles down at my brother. "Joey ... thanks again for remembering to open up the windows. That was very responsible, and with such a big house, I need all the help I can get."

What about me? I'm helpful. Those *rosquillos* are from scratch, for gosh sakes.

I flop back onto the sofa and glare at Dad as he heads off down the hall. It doesn't take long before I start feeling guilty. Maybe I shouldn't be so touchy. He just knows that the windows got opened, not that I nagged Joey into doing it.

Feeling slightly better about myself, I hop up from the sofa and head for the kitchen to check the cookies. At least we have the Internet now. Maybe getting away from our old house will start Dad writing again. Author of five-and-a-half historical novels about the kings and queens of Spain, he hasn't written a thing since Mom died. When she was around, money from her catering business took care of the bills when Dad got his writer's block. With no money coming in, we started to get letters. First, about credit card bills, later for the overdue mortgage. That's why we ended up here. Free rent.

I walk by the dining room and hit the brakes. The room is dark, and the curtains are flapping in the breeze. "Joey," I call back to him. "Why didn't you open the curtains when you opened the dining room window?"

"I did open the curtains."

"Obviously not."

Joey swings himself over the back of the sofa and scoots into the dining room on blue socked feet. I follow.

"I pulled them open with this cord . . ." His hand slips behind the thick green drapes and they slide open, exposing cracked windows framed with cobwebs. "Then, I turned that crank as far as it would go."

"Maybe a ghost closed the curtains." It sure pushed that powdered sugar box around easily enough.

"Dad says ghosts aren't real."

"Maybe they aren't . . . maybe they are." But seeing as there's no reason Dad would have shut them, that only leaves two explanations: One, Joey only thinks he opened them or two, a ghost really did close them—why, I have no clue.

Like most kids with Asperger's, Joey's always one hundred percent honest. Knowing he'd pass a lie detector test if asked *and* that my open-minded ideas about ghosts will get back to Dad if I argue the point, I drop the subject and peer out the window at a huge backyard.

Untended since Grandma died, it's filled with half-dead grass and overgrown shrubs and trees. But Joey couldn't care less about those things. It's the swimming pool that catches his eye. He squashes his nose to the glass, and a rare smile crosses his lips. If the water was clean, he'd probably be splashing in it right now. I love swimming too, but in rivers or the ocean. Something about pools has always given me the creeps. Maybe it's the way I can see my reflection in the still blue water. It's almost as though there's another me in there.

"I bet Mom swam in that pool a lot," Joey says.

Yeah, probably. I let out a sigh. "Don't worry. You'll swim in it someday, just like she did." I stare at the shallow moss-covered swamp and try to imagine the pool back when Mom was a kid. Did she play Marco Polo with her friends or dive for weight rings like kids do today?

My happy thoughts fade when I notice something in the water. "What's that?"

"Where?"

"Over by the far wall. That dark shape. It's this big." I hold my hands two feet apart.

"I see leaves and a plastic bag."

Again, my chest tightens. "Look . . . it's over there . . ." I tap the glass with my finger. "Just under the surface."

"Are you talking about the diving board's shadow?"

"No, not the stupid shadow. Are you—?" Teasing? He can't be. He doesn't know how.

I take a step back, ready to leave. "Never mind."

Back in the kitchen, I quickly forget the pool and whatever I saw floating beneath its surface. I've got more important things to worry about, like frosting these cookies and facing all those new kids and teachers at school tomorrow.

CHAPTER 2

MY FIRST MORNING at Sierra Middle School isn't the worst, but it isn't the best either. Like some lost tourist, I wander the campus, map glued to my hand. In lit class a tall girl says hi as I walk to my seat. In ceramics class, a boy asks to borrow my rolling pin. Other than that, I'm pretty much invisible.

After ceramics comes lunch. Unlike my old school where we all stayed in the cafeteria, here everyone eats outside unless it's raining. With no clouds in the sky, the entire seventh grade population is scattered across the courtyard, either out on the grass or sitting at picnic tables on the large covered patio.

I work my way through the food line, then step out into the bright sunshine, happy I decided to wear shorts. At least I'm dressed like everyone else.

Some of the tables are full, but there are still plenty of empty seats. Chicken nuggets in hand, I drift through the patio area, hoping some kind strangers will invite me to sit with them. Since I met my three best friends back in kindergarten, I never dealt with stuff like this back at my old school.

Knowing that finding someone to eat with is just another part of my day-long audition, I mosey past table after table, trying to put out the right vibe. Hopefully it's halfway between bashful and stuck-up. One table is filled with girls, and their chatter reminds me of my group back home. Heart pounding, I try my best to make eye contact, but they're in their own world. Talk about self-absorbed. Is that how I acted around new kids?

At the next table, two out of three people look up. One

even smiles. They look nice enough, but the problem is, they're all boys. No way I'm ready for that. I smile back but keep walking.

It isn't long before I circle the entire patio. Nobody else looks up. Nobody calls me over. Now what? I can't just sit down and say hi. Not up for doing a second lap, I grab the closest empty table and start eating my once warm chicken nuggets.

Yeah, chicken. You are what you eat, right?

With nobody to talk to, the nuggets go down fast, and pretty soon I'm gathering up my trash. As I head to the garbage can, it hits me. Oh my gosh! This is Joey's first day too. Now who's self-absorbed? I slump back to my table, wondering how he's doing. Hopefully, his new teacher is as good as the one he had before.

With nobody to vent my frustrations to, I start fidgeting. There must be something I can do. If it were up to me, I'd trot into the cafeteria kitchen and whip up a batch of chocolate chip cookies. Since I'm sure the cooks would frown on that, I settle on a visit to the library. Maybe I can find something that explains all the weird stuff going on in our house.

For the tenth time today, I pull out my school map. For the second time today, it's a blur. I pull off my glasses. Great. Before it was clay from art class. Now it's chicken grease.

Feeling like a total dork, I clean my lenses then scan the map for the library. If I'm reading it right, the library is just past the auditorium on the left. I shuffle past a row of orange lockers and some boys putting up Spanish club posters. The air conditioning feels good as I step through the doors.

"Hi there," says a chunky grandma type pushing a cart full of books. "Just browsing, or are you researching a particular subject?"

Researching? Well, maybe not that, but—before I know it, the word pops out. "Ghosts?"

"A popular subject. You'll find them in the nonfiction area, section 130."

Nonfiction? Really? I take my time and stroll across what I hope won't become my permanent lunchtime hangout.

Actually, that wouldn't be so bad. This library is much nicer than the one at my other school. It's bigger, newer. Instead of mold and mildew, it smells like cinnamon. There are lots of cute posters on the walls and more than one snuggly looking chair to curl up in with a good paperback. I saunter down the aisle, eyes narrowed on the book spines and their little white labels. Okay, there's 120 . . . 126 . . . 128.

Section 130 does not disappoint. There must be at least twenty books on ghosts and tons more on other goofy stuff like the Loch Ness Monster, Bigfoot, even the Chupacabra. To take up time, I decide to read all the titles.

The Complete Book of Werewolves, stupid. *How to Hold a Séance*, better. *Haunted Government Buildings of Northern California*, better yet. Great choices for bedtime reading. Dad will be so thrilled when I wake him up screaming at three o'clock in the morning.

"That one's my favorite," a female voice says behind me.

I spin around. Holy crabs!

With her so tall and me so close, I feel like I'm standing next to a redwood tree. I tip my head back and discover a friendly heart-shaped face surrounded by wavy auburn hair. I know her. She's the tall girl from literature class. The one who said hi to me.

"I'm sorry. Did I frighten you?" Her accent is cool. British.

"Maybe a little." Geez, she's even taller than Dad. I catch myself staring and look away. "Guess I was really into these book titles."

"You're Theresa Martinez, right? My aunt suggested I speak with you."

"What?" I take a step back. "How'd you know my name, and who's your aunt?"

A flush creeps across her cheeks. "Sorry, that sounded

a bit mysterious, didn't it?" She hunches down a bit. "I'm Kerry Addison. My aunt is Amelia Lacey, the real estate agent your folks hired to sell your grandmother's house a few years back. Since we're both new to Fern Creek, she suggested I look you up. I'd love to chat with you about your house—if you have the time."

Okay, I remember Mom and Dad trying to sell the place. But why is this girl so interested in some old—wait . . . didn't she say something about that one ghost book being her favorite?

With the librarian already giving us the stink eye for talking so much, we head to the far end of the library to find an empty table. Like me, Kerry's wearing shorts too. She motions for me to sit and drops into the chair across from me. Immediately, I'm jealous of the long legs stretching out in front of her.

"So, have you seen any ghosts yet?" she whispers.

I knew it. "Is that why you came looking for me, because you think my house is haunted?"

"Partly, but I really am new to the area. Three weeks ago, my family and I were flying across the Atlantic Ocean."

Okay, then what makes her think we have ghosts? I raise my chin. "Where do you buy your groceries?"

"Pardon?"

"Is it that little market on Peach Street? Because there's an old white-haired lady working there, and she thinks our house is haunted too."

"That's interesting, but I didn't hear about it from any old ladies, white-haired or otherwise."

"Then who told you about the house?"

"My aunt. It's why she couldn't sell the place. She did things to frighten away the clients."

"That's crazy. Why would your aunt want to frighten away the—?"

"Not my aunt. The ghost. Nothing terribly bad, just . . . disturbing. Taking things. Closing doors. Once she hid a woman's purse, and it took most of an hour to find it."

"She? Who's *she*?" Please don't say it's Grandma Carmen. Please don't say—

"Your grandmother, of course."

Aw, geez! No wonder Mom and Dad quit trying to sell the place. I slump down in my chair and start chewing my lip. But why would Grandma haunt her own house? That's the kind of stuff you hear about on TV, not real life.

All I can think to say is, "I haven't *seen* any ghosts."

"Perhaps not an actual manifestation, but you must have seen or heard *something*. Maybe an odd thump or a creak in the night?"

Of course, I think of the powdered sugar. Like one of those popcorn thingies stuck between your teeth that your tongue can't leave alone, I've gone over it in my head a hundred times, and it only happened yesterday.

She must see it on my face because she pats my arm. "Oh, please tell."

Kerry's pleading eyes remind me of Mittens, our neighbor's cat back home. Every time Dad barbecued, Mittens would turn up, scamming for a scrap of chicken or steak. A fuzzy little conman, he would rub against my leg and stare up at me until I fed him.

Like Mittens, it's hard not to give Kerry what she wants. "Okay, there was *one* thing, but it's really no big deal. Yesterday I was getting ready to make some cookies, and I couldn't find the powdered sugar." Oh, geez. I clench my jaw. I can't believe I'm telling her this.

"A lot like Aunt Amelia's purse story," she says, her voice starting to get wheezy. She picks up her backpack and gestures for me to continue.

Continue? She sounds like the dog that swallowed a whistle in that old cartoon. "You . . . you sure you're okay?" I wait as she pulls an asthma inhaler from the front zipper pocket and sucks in a couple of puffs.

"It's mostly for dust," she says, already sounding stronger, "but sometimes I need it when I'm excited. Go on, finish your story."

Once Kerry breathes easier, I relax too, and after a bit, I've not only told her about the sugar, but also the thing with Joey and the dining room curtains. By the time I'm finished, a big grin stretches across her face.

She sits up straight. "You know, I chase ghosts."

"Really?" It comes out more sarcastic than I like, and I bite my lip when I realize I just sounded like Dad. Who cares if Kerry's super into ghosts? I watch cooking shows all the time. Does that make me crazy? "How many have you seen?" I ask, hoping I come off less bratty this time.

"None here in the States, but back in England I saw a shadow figure *and* I heard quite a few odd noises up in my gran's attic. Believe it or not, your house is practically new compared to some of the homes back in England. With so many people dying over the years it's not unusual for the odd one to hang back."

Not sure if I agree, I nod anyway. That's when I notice Kerry has one brown eye and one green Hmm. That's another thing she has in common with Mittens.

Kerry smirks. "I see you've noticed my eyes."

"Sorry. Didn't mean to stare. Actually, I like them. They're . . . unique."

"That's okay. I used to hate them until Grandmother Addison let me in on the big secret. Her eyes are mismatched too, and according to her, 'it facilitates one's communication with spirits.'"

Whoa! "That's a pretty cool skill. Have you ever used it?"

"I've tried a few times, but the ghosts weren't interested. Takes quite a bit of effort on their part, you know."

Makes sense. "That's what they say on *Ghosters* too."

"Once I perfect it, I plan to use that skill to become the youngest person to ever document a paranormal manifestation. I even have some of the equipment the chaps on TV use." She reaches into her backpack and pulls out something the size and shape of a TV remote. "This came in the post last week. It's an EMF meter. That stands for—"

"Electromagnetic field. The guys on *Ghosters* use one. It lights up when spirits are around." Okay, so besides cooking shows, I watch paranormal stuff too. But I never take them seriously. For me, it's all about getting scared. It's fun when you're safe in your own living room.

As I'm talking, Kerry tips her head to the side and starts to smile.

"What? Is this some sort of prank on the new kid?"

"No, no." She shakes her head and grins even harder. "It's just that at first I tracked you down because of your house. But I really like you. You seem to know a lot about spirits, plus, you're brave. Most people would have run off like a frightened squirrel when that sugar box fell off the counter."

"Come on. I was totally freaked."

"Yes, but you stayed. I think we'd make good partners."

"Partners in what? Crime?"

She waves me off. "Ghost chasing, silly. And we'd start by searching your house together." Her hand flies to her mouth. "Sorry, was that too forward?"

Well, kind of. But who cares? Afraid of running off my first possible friend, I say, "No, it sounds fun. Got any more ghost chasing stuff in there?"

With a devilish grin, she slides her chair as close to mine as possible. "Right now all I have is this, but I ordered an EVP recorder a couple of weeks ago from a brilliant website called Ghoststuff.com. It should arrive any day. I've already started saving for a full spectrum video recorder."

Yeah, I've heard of those. Wish I could remember what they do.

Kerry leans back, arms crossed. "It may take a year, but when I'm finished, my ghost-chasing kit is going to be just as good as they have on *Ghosters*, maybe better."

That is so cool. "Where do you get the money?"

"Babysitting."

"What? My dad would never leave me alone with my little brother. He says I'm too young."

She laughs. "That's probably because your brother is an angel compared to our Robert. He's barely four and absolutely horrid. Mum calls their times apart her mental health breaks." She throws up her hands. "Forget all that. When can we search your house?"

Yeah, when? Dad thinks anything to do with ghosts is stupid. "Let me talk to my dad tonight. If he's okay with it, you can come over for dinner tomorrow. We'll worry about the searching business later."

Satisfied, Kerry smiles back like a kid who just heard she's going to Disneyland.

CHAPTER 3

THE SCHOOL IS only two blocks from our house, so I walk home after my last class. Late September, the sun is already low and the shadow of my grandparents' huge Victorian looms over everything, including me.

I wonder what Mom would think if she knew we'd moved in here. It's no wonder Kerry wants to explore it. The inside might look okay, but outside it's a place you'd only enter on a dare.

Chipped and peeling paint, cracked windows. The only sign of life is a hose snaking out across the balding brown yard and the sprinkler swinging slowly back and forth, Dad's shot at getting the grass to grow back. As I crunch my way down the gravel driveway, something catches my eye at the far end of the house. I head over.

Back before everything fell apart, I expected to find Dad parked in front of his computer when I got home from school. As a writer, it was normal for him to spend most of his day there, working on his latest book. But that's all ancient history. Since then, the only place my father spends his afternoons is on the sofa, so it's a big surprise when I find him up on a ladder, hacking away at the honeysuckle vines that have taken over half of the front porch.

I step across what passes for our front lawn and drop my backpack beside me. "Nice work, but it's going to take a lot more than a little pruning to get this place right."

He keeps cutting. "Well, you've got to prune before you can paint. I told you nobody's lived here for seven years. What did you expect?"

"I never expected this. Look at those broken shutters—and the yard. Half the stuff is dead and the other half . . ." The Dad-annoying words fly out before I can stop them. Stupid, stupid, stupid. I should be happy he's doing something besides sleeping.

Finished with cutting the low stuff, he moves up a step. The ladder wobbles with every chop, cut, and snip.

"Joey's first day at school didn't go well," he says between hacks. "You should talk to him."

I was afraid that would happen. I grab hold of the ladder and try to steady it for him. "Okay, but don't you want to know how *my* first day went?"

"Oh, yeah." He pauses in the chopping and looks down at me. "Sorry. How'd it go?"

"Pretty good, actually." Anxious to tell him about Kerry, I rush through my list of classes and get down to the good stuff. "Her name is Kerry. She's British."

"*¿Inglesa?*" He hacks through an ivy branch, and it lands on my shoe.

"Yeah, her aunt was our real estate agent. Andrea . . . Angela . . ."

"Amelia Lacey?"

"Yeah, that's her."

"I remember her. When she couldn't sell the house she blamed it on ghosts." He shakes his head. "What a whack job."

Get it all out. "That's funny, because Kerry thinks the house is haunted too."

"Oh, really?" He steps off the ladder and moves it a few feet over. "Must run in the family. Maybe they're related to that woman in the grocery store too."

"I really doubt that. But she is anxious to see inside the house." Before he can climb back up the ladder, I grab his arm. "Is it okay if I invite her over for dinner?"

"If she's anything like her aunt, she probably expects to find ghosts roaming the hallways."

I smile. "Yeah, probably, but can she come? I was thinking maybe tomorrow." Please, please, please.

"I suppose." The way my dad is staring at the place you'd think it was a Beverly Hills mansion. "You know, back when your grandparents lived here, this was the nicest house on the block. The paint was fresh, the yards were always manicured, front and back . . ." His eyes cloud over as if remembering something unpleasant. "If I could just get that book finished, then we wouldn't have to worry about money, and—"

Arg! That stupid writer's block. I fill my cheeks with air, blow it out. "You will, Dad. Just . . . give it time."

"Time, right." Frowning, he strides across the yard toward the big wheeled garbage tote which he rolls up alongside the pile of clippings.

Even though I can't tell whether he likes me helping or not, I spend the next few minutes gathering up what he's chopping down. The house really does need work, but instead of more idiotic complaining, I try a more positive approach. "It would be cheaper if we fix some of the problems ourselves. Painting is easy, and we could learn how to replace the cracked windows by watching do-it-yourself videos on YouTube. In fact . . ." Up in one of the third floor windows, a curtain flutters. "Is that Joey?"

Dad looks at me sideways. "Don't tell me you're seeing ghosts now."

I point up toward the third floor. "No, really. There, in that tower thingy. The curtain moved like somebody was pulling it back to look out." Somebody like Grandma Carmen . . . ?

Dad smirks and follows my finger with his gaze. "Like you said, Theresa, the window's cracked. It's just the breeze getting through . . . a draft."

I toss my arms up in frustration. "But I saw *something.*"

He turns back to his bushes, and I scowl at the back of his head. OMG, that man is so closed-minded.

Joey must have heard my voice, because he runs around the side of the house and stands next to Dad, rake balanced on his shoulder. Joey's more than a foot shorter than Dad, so they're a bizarre set of twins: same ruler-straight dark hair, same big brown eyes, only one tall and buff, the other small and bony. Nothing like me.

"What were you guys talking about?"

Since Joey accepts everything as is, I doubt if he would blink twice if he found Grandma Carmen's ghost dragging the sprinkler around the front yard. But Dad's right there, so, instead of ghosts, I say, "We were talking about the new friend I made in school today. She's Br—" Before the words finish coming out of my mouth, I want to suck them back in. And not because of Dad.

Joey's knuckles turn white as he squeezes the rake handle. "I didn't make any friends today."

I'm such a dope. As tough as all the new changes have been for me, they're twice as hard for Joey. It wasn't until last year that he finally made a friend, and now Trent is all the way back in Crescent City.

Dad gives me a "fix it" look, as he's done so many times in the last six months.

"Come on, Jojo." I take the rake and pass it to Dad. "Let's go inside."

At first Joey hangs back, but I reach for his hand, and he runs up the sagging wooden stairs leading to the front porch. If you want Joey to move, try touching him.

The door is unlocked, and we step into the large entryway. Dust particles bob and sway in the light like tiny dancers in a spotlight.

"This room," he waves his arms in the same *ta-da* flourish Dad used the day we moved in, "is called the foyer." Funny. Outside, Joey was ready to cry, but as I'd hoped, the change of scenery seems to have cleared all that from his mind. At least for now.

"Are you making a joke?" I ask. With him it's hard to tell.

"I think so. Was I funny?"

"Hilarious. You have Dad down perfectly."

He looks at the floor. "Down?"

I smile. "Sorry, it means that you acted just like him."

"Good." He starts for the living room, then stops. "If Mom was alive, Dad would have finished his book by now." He pounds his clenched fists against his thighs, emphasizing our parents' names. "Then we would all still be living in our old house, and I'd still be back at my old school with my old teachers and my best buddy, Trent."

If, if, if. God, I hate when he gets like this. Still, it's hard to get mad when I have the same thoughts.

Even though Joey would be fine with me talking to the back of his head, I'm not, so I circle around. He's crying, but since he doesn't like touching unless it's his idea, I can't hug him, and the space between us stays empty.

It's times like these that I miss Mom the most. She died on her way to pick up my birthday present. Sometimes I worry Dad blames me for it. Heck, I blame myself. If I wasn't so particular about which saucepans I wanted she wouldn't have been anywhere near Chef World, and that stupid teenager would have crashed into somebody else.

A lousy substitute, tears fill my eyes as I struggle to find the words Mom might have used. "You'll make another friend, Jojo. And you'll get used to everything else, too . . . the house . . . the teachers. After a few days it'll all be part of your routine."

I guess that's what he needs to hear, because his hands slowly relax, and his expression changes from "I hate it" to looking totally confused. I consider it progress.

Like every other day since we've lived here, he cuts through the living room and over to the huge marble fireplace. On the mantel is a treasure-trove of old family photos placed there years ago. Joey always focuses on the one of Grandma and Grandpa Ramos, my parents' wedding picture, and the two from when I was a baby. But his favorite is a five by seven of Mom back in high school, dressed up as a Spanish flamenco dancer.

"She looks nice in that dress," he tells me. *"Muy guapa."*

"She sure does."

"You look like her."

He's told me that at least five times in the last few days, but I let it pass.

"You have the same curly hair. Same green eyes."

At his last school they were teaching Joey to read facial expressions, so I slap on a big smile and turn so he can see it. "Guess that means you think I'm pretty too, huh?"

For a second an embarrassed smile crosses his lips. I'll take it.

Joey's new routine is to look at each picture and comment. Usually it's one word, like handsome, or pretty. This time he surprises me by picking up the two baby pictures of me, one in each hand. "How come there are two of you, but none of me?"

"Guess Mom didn't send them one."

"But why didn't she?"

"You know why."

"No, not really." Joey studies the two photos as if they're *Highlights* picture puzzles, and the explanation is hidden somewhere in plain sight.

You're not going to find the answer there, hermanito. "Look," I tell him. "Dad stuck all our old pictures up in the hall closet. If you want, we could switch one of my baby pictures for one of yours. Want to?"

"Maybe later." He sets the photos down and turns toward the stairs. "I'm going to my room to play some games." But instead of dashing off, he stands there. "My old room had blue carpeting." His bottom lip quivers, making him look closer to five than ten. "I miss that blue carpeting."

A knot forms in my throat. "Me too, Jojo, but this is our home now."

Hard to think of a place as home when everything in it belonged to people you don't remember meeting. Not expecting much, I reach out my hand. To my surprise, he takes it, and we walk all the way up the stairs before he shakes me off.

There are nine doors in the upstairs hallway, four on each side and one on the end, to the right of the servants' stairs. The same wood paneling on the walls downstairs covers the bottom half of these.

When we moved in, Dad showed us Mom's old room, second from the end on the right. Joey hated the pink flowered wallpaper, but for me, there was no other choice. The chance to sleep in Mom's old bed made selling all our old furniture tolerable. Plus, it was as close as I would ever get to hanging out with her again. Without opening the door, Joey picked the room across from me. I think he was a little scared about living in such a big house. I was too. Sometimes I still am.

That's not to say we never peeked into any other rooms. We did, but how many old chenille bedspreads can a kid stand to look at?

"Want to check out some more rooms?" I ask, hoping to keep Joey off his video games for a little while.

He opens his door. "Not really. Dad just bought me a new game. Want to play it?"

What? I get my cell phone taken away to save money, and Joey gets a new game? God, that's so like Dad. "No thanks." With my lips pressed into a tight smile, I step past Joey and pull open the next door. Cold air leaks out, along with a hint of perfume.

Joey holds his nose. "Yuck. Now I *really* don't want to go in there."

"That's weird." I rub at the newly sprouted goose bumps on my arms. Nobody's lived here since Grandma Carmen died. Has that smell been trapped in there all that time?

He steps over and stares into the darkness. "Do smells just hang around forever?"

"How would I know?" Wait . . . didn't Joey air out all the rooms?

Joey shuts the door. "No more smelling rooms. Come play with me."

Since it's not Joey's fault Dad favors him, I say, "Only if *you* check out that room at the end of the hall with me first."

I traipse over and jiggle the knob a few times, then give the door a kick when it doesn't open.

Joey tugs on my sleeve. "Are you mad at the door?"

"Huh?" The door, no. Dad, on the other hand . . . I blow out a frustrated breath. "No, I . . . don't worry about it."

Theresa.

Less than a whisper.

I whirl around. Besides us, the hallway is empty. "Did you hear that, Jojo?"

"What?"

All of a sudden my chest aches and I feel like crying. What's wrong with me? I was thinking about the door, not Mom.

"Theresa! Joey!" our dad shouts up to us. "Are you hungry? Let's go get some burgers."

With that, all the sad feelings vanish, gone so fast I wonder if I really had them. I glance back at the door. I turn around, and Joey is already halfway down the stairs.

CHAPTER 4

KERRY COMES OVER the next evening just as I'm getting ready to roll out the dough I've been kneading.

"Hiya, what are you making?" she asks. "Tortillas?"

"Pizza dough. Once I put on the sauce and cheese I'm going to top it with pepperoni, black olives, and arugula."

"What's arugula?"

"This." I pass her a plastic bag full of the stuff. "All the big chefs use it."

"Ah, we call it rocket back in England. I've never seen it on pizza." Her eyes narrow. "You sure these aren't dandelion leaves?"

"Pretty sure." I lead her over to the big wooden cutting board and hand her a chef's knife. "Since I'm assembling the pizza, you get to chop up some stuff for the salad."

"Isn't this a punishment in the army?" she asks, knife dangling between her thumb and index finger.

"I believe that's peeling potatoes. What's wrong? Not into cooking?"

She peers around the kitchen. "Not as much as you, obviously, but don't fret. I'm totally willing to help out."

For the next few minutes the kitchen goes quiet as we focus on our work. Kerry slices the cucumber while I roll out the pizza dough and pour on a jar of sauce. Mom would have cringed at the sight of me using store-bought, but with school and homework, I have to be realistic.

"You seem to know what you're doing," Kerry says. "Did your mum teach you?"

"Yeah, ever since I could hold a spoon. She had me frosting cupcakes when I was three." A walnut-sized lump rises in the back of my throat, as it's done a million times in the last few months. I turn away from Kerry and spend some time staring into the refrigerator. Think of something else. Drink something. There's half a can of Pepsi sitting on a shelf. I take a few swigs and the lump shrinks down. Relieved, I slide open a wobbly vegetable drawer and pull out some celery for the salad.

"I don't know what I would do if my mum died," Kerry says. She cuts off a couple of stalks and steps to the sink to wash them. "You miss her a lot, don't you?"

"Heck yeah. I just wish I had a chance to tell her I loved her before she . . ." My voice cracks. "You know?" God, I hate when this happens.

Looking a little embarrassed, she nods and focuses on the celery.

I thought I had it under control back at the fridge, but the lump is back, and now it's the size of a kiwi. If I talk I'll cry, so there's an uncomfortable minute as I get myself together.

Finally, Kerry clears her throat and says, "I've been thinking about the ghost."

"Yeah?" I croak. I peer over at her celery slices. They're uneven, but I keep my mouth shut, thankful for the topic change.

"Yes, if we get a good recording we can enter it in that contest they're always talking about on *Ghosters*. Two hundred thousand is a lot of money, even if we split it."

Our recording? Of what? A box of sugar falling off the kitchen counter? I'm not nearly as closed-minded as Dad, but for all I know there really was an earthquake. Like he says, everything has a logical explanation when it comes down to it. I watch Kerry as she moves on to the mushrooms. She really believes all this ghost stuff. It must be nice.

"Yeah," I say, playing along. "If we win, we'll have more than enough money to fix up the house. That stove works okay, but Mom had a real professional model back at our old place." Forget the renovations, what about paying bills? I can't remember the last time Dad actually wrote something. All he uses his computer for now is checking e-mails.

"Your mum must have prepared all sorts of lovely Mexican dishes with a stove like that. Tacos . . . burritos . . ."

I sprinkle two fat handfuls of shredded mozzarella onto the pizza and smile. "Oh, I get it. We have dark hair and our last name is Martinez, so you assume we're Mexican."

"You're not?"

"No, my grandparents came from Spain—both sides. I'll make tacos for you next time, if you want."

"Are you saying tacos aren't Spanish?" she asks, looking confused.

"Nope. Burritos either." I waggle my hand at her. "Hey, it's no big deal. Lots of people think that. It used to drive my mom nuts." Again I tear up, but since I can't spend my life staring into the refrigerator, I grab a couple of tissues.

"Did you ask your dad if we could explore the house for ghosts?" Kerry asks, ignoring my drama.

I was wondering when she'd get back to that. "No way," I tell her. "He'd think it was stupid."

Her lower lip juts out in a pout.

"Don't worry, we're still doing it. We're just going to be—"

"Sneaky?"

"I was going to say stealthy."

WE EAT IN the kitchen. As usual, Dad and Joey sit across from me. I hoped Dad would wear something nice, but he keeps on his usual sloppy t-shirt and running pants, even though he never walks farther than the mailbox.

Kerry takes the empty chair to my right and watches, eyebrows arched, as Joey dissects his pizza slice. Every ingredient is carefully separated from the rest, organized according to how soon he plans to eat it. His favorite, pepperoni, gets a front row seat, followed by crust wiped clean of sauce, cheese, and his least favorite, the olive slices.

Since Joey won't eat anything green, he mounds the arugula on his napkin. I can't tell what Kerry's thinking, but maybe that's a good thing.

"So, Kerry," Dad says once we've all loaded our plates, "I hear you're from England."

Kerry blushes. "Is the accent that obvious? I wish I could lose it."

"Don't," Joey says. "It's different. Pretty."

Worried he'd say something embarrassing, I tried to prepare Joey for Kerry's visit by telling him about the accent, as well as how super tall she is. Who'd have guessed he'd turn out to be Mister Suave?

The one I didn't think to prepare is Kerry. She focuses on her plate for a few moments, then smiles up at Joey. "Want to hear something funny? When Theresa told me your dad was a writer I didn't recognize the name, so last night I looked him up on Amazon." She gives Dad a lopsided grin. "You've written quite a few books."

Since the last one was published eight months ago, I stare at Dad to see how he'll react.

He sits back and sighs. "That's true, but I'm no Ken Follett."

Who in the heck is Ken Follett?

Kerry's chin dips down. "I don't know who that is, but anyone who's managed to get five books published must be good at it."

"I wasn't referring to my writing skills." Dad fans his hand at the old stove, the dented fridge. "It's success I'm talking about . . . the sales."

Uh oh. Money talk. Well, at least he's speaking about it now. Two months ago, he wouldn't even answer the phone when his agent called. Hopefully Kerry won't ask if he's—

"Working on anything new?"

"Uh . . . maybe." He peers across at me, chin raised. "Theresa . . . ?"

Great. He probably thinks I put her up to it.

" . . . why don't you give your guest a tour of the house after dinner? Kerry, you're anxious to see a ghost, right?"

Whaaaaaat? I gasp, a bad thing to do with a mouthful of pizza. With pepperoni lodged in my windpipe, I form a T with my hands, calling for time. After a string of coughs and gasps, I finally suck in enough air to speak. "Come on, Dad. You believe in ghosts like I believe in the tooth fairy. What are you up to?"

"Nothing. Kerry thinks the house is haunted, and it seems that everyone else in town does too. What better way to prove it isn't? You can look anywhere but the third floor."

"Ha!" I elbow Kerry. "That won't be a problem. I don't even know how to get up there."

"It's the big door at the end of the hall," Joey tells me. "The one you got mad at yesterday. Remember? You started kicking it."

Thanks a lot, Jojo. As heat fills my cheeks, I look from Dad to Kerry, face scrunched with embarrassment. "I wasn't really kicking it, I was just trying to—"

"Get it open?" Dad narrows his eyes on me. "The door is locked, and it's going to stay that way."

"Why? Was Grandma Carmen a serial killer and that's where she stashed all the bodies?"

I'm joking, but from the surprised look on his face, you'd think I just guessed the truth.

"No," he tells me, once he's recovered. "Your grandparents always kept that part of the house closed off. It cost too much to heat, and since they weren't using the space, they never bothered to fix it up."

"I wanna see it," Joey says, folding the arugula into his napkin.

I gulp down some soda. "Yeah, it sounds cool."

"It's not cool." Dad leans toward me, his eyes narrowed. "I don't want you kids going in there. The floor was already dangerous when your grandparents bought the house. If you went up there now you'd fall right through and get badly hurt . . . or worse."

"What do you mean by worse?" Joey asks.

"Dead."

Joey pops his last slice of pepperoni into his mouth. "That *is* bad."

As if somebody flicked a switch, Dad sits back. His serious face is gone, replaced by a halfhearted grin. "Heck, even if I wanted to take you up there, I can't. I haven't found the key."

"I don't mind," Kerry says, "I'm happy to see any part of your home. How about you, Joey? Care to come along?"

Joey picks up his crust and says, "No, thank you."

I clear my throat. "Joey always watches his bug DVDs after dinner."

"Well," Dad says, "maybe, just this once, he could skip the DVDs. What do you say, Jojo? Think you can leave the TV alone for an hour?" He waits until Joey meets his eyes.

"They're not about bugs," Joey says. "They're on insects and arachnids. And yes, I can go one hour without them." Although he remembers to make the corners of his mouth go up, his jaw is clenched—a sure sign he'd rather not.

Kerry grins. "What if we actually do see a ghost, Mr. Martinez?"

Dad smiles his oh-you're-so-young smile and picks up his glass. "That, Kerry, is something I'm not worried about."

Everyone laughs except Joey, who's been studying Kerry's face all through dinner.

Noticing, she says, "I like the way you eat your pizza, Joey."

His gaze falls back to his plate. When he doesn't answer, I reach under the table and tap his leg with my foot.

After a few seconds, Joey looks up at Kerry and says, "Thank you. I like how your eyes are two different colors."

Ghost chasing is going to be interesting.

CHAPTER 5

BACK BEFORE MOM died, Dad would always put in at least an hour of writing after dinner. These days, he spends his evenings flopped on the recliner, watching baseball, leaving me and Joey to clean up. Kerry helps, and since there's no dishwasher, we do everything by hand. Once everything is washed and put away, I toss my dish towel onto the kitchen counter.

"This is your big chance, Kerry. What do you want to see first?"

She tips her head toward the wooden door next to the avocado green refrigerator. "Is that the basement?"

The basement. Great. Even though that's where the washer and dryer are, I haven't been down there yet. There's no lock on the door, just a bolt to hold it shut.

Joey slides the bolt and pulls the door open with a creak. "It's extremely dark down there."

Taller than Joey by more than a foot, Kerry peers over his head. "Perfect, that's exactly what we want. Got a torch handy?"

"You kidding?" I imagine Kerry leading the way, flaming torch in hand.

She bites her lip. "Sorry, I forgot they're called flashlights here."

"This house is old," Joey says, "but it does have electricity."

"Of course, but traditionally, one looks for ghosts in the dark. They never use lights on *Ghosters*."

I giggle. "I don't want to be mean, but why didn't *you* bring a flashlight?"

Kerry's shoulders slump. "My brother ran down the batteries."

"No problem. I think I saw some in a drawer." While I search, Kerry heads off to get her EMF meter. By the time I track down the flashlights she's back in the kitchen waving the little black box out in front of her.

"Dad's not going to like you taking his TV remote," Joey tells her.

She paces the room, arm outstretched. "It might as well be a remote, for all the good it's doing."

"That's an EMF meter," I explain to Joey. "A ghost detecting tool. Kerry must expect the kitchen to be crawling with them."

My brother scans the linoleum for ghosts until Kerry pulls her cell phone from her back pocket. "Kerry," he says, eyeing her phone, "even if ghosts do exist, I doubt if they accept phone calls—or texts for that matter."

"I wasn't planning on . . ." She studies Joey's blank expression. "Like most mobile telephones, this one's got a video camera. Not the best, but who knows? Maybe we'll get lucky."

Joey crinkles his brow, and we wait as he chooses his words. "Oh, I get it. You want to document what we see."

"Right."

For a moment, he meets Kerry's eyes. "Can I be in the one to work it?"

She shrugs. "I don't see why not. I can't very well monitor the EMF meter and film ghosts at the same time." She passes him the cell phone. "Who knows, maybe you'll capture images good enough for the *Ghosters* contest."

"What's that?" Joey asks.

"It's a contest that pays a lot of money to whoever captures the best images of a ghost."

As if to remind me of how broke we are, the ancient refrigerator clicks on with a loud *whomp.* I cut my eyes at it. The only way that antique gets replaced is if we really *do* win the contest.

I flick the flashlights on and off, then pass one to Kerry. "Here's your *torch.* What do we do now?"

"We turn off the lights and start working our way down."

Hmmm. Creeping around in a dark basement. Did I actually think this would be fun? With a sigh, I drag over one of the kitchen chairs.

"What on earth are you doing?" Kerry asks.

I swing the basement door open and shove the chair up against it, propping it wide. "If we're going to do this, the kitchen lights stay on. That way we'll be able to see it if something happens down there."

Kerry blinks. "Why? What do you think will happen?"

"Theresa's scared of the dark," Joey says as his fingers work the cell phone.

"What?" I realize my mouth is hanging open and snap it shut. Joey, you big mouth. "I'm not scared, I just—"

"You asked Dad to put a night light in the hallway upstairs."

"Okay, fine. Joey's right. But I'm not scared so much when it's dark-*ish*. It's the dark-dark that really gets me, you know? Like when you can't see a thing." I cross my arms and look at Kerry. Okay, go ahead and laugh.

Instead, she reaches through the basement doorway and flicks the light switch.

"Darn, it doesn't work," she mutters.

"What's the problem?" Joey asks. "You said ghost-chasers don't use lights anyway."

"I was hoping to give Theresa a little preview of what she's getting herself into."

Aw. Is it just Kerry, or are all British people this considerate? I throw back my shoulders and click on my flashlight. "Okay, let's do this."

CHAPTER 6

FROM UPSTAIRS LOOKING down, the basement is just creepy. But once I go down a few steps, I realize I'm not just leaving the light of the kitchen, I'm leaving its safety too. For all I know, this darkness is filled with horrible creatures waiting to snatch me up and swallow me whole. I take a deep breath and slowly blow it out. In this dim light Joey seems calm, almost bored.

Not nearly as anxious to get down there as Kerry, I take one step at a time.

Why does she have to be into ghosts?

Step.

Why couldn't it be cooking?

Step.

Halfway down, I stop, draw in another deep breath. Directly in front of us, the flashlight shows a big wooden shelf stocked with dusty jars of canned tomatoes. Nothing scary there, but what about the rest of the place?

"Think I'll check for monsters," I tell them. Only half kidding, I lean against the railing, peer over.

"See any?" Joey asks, serious as ever.

Since I don't want Kerry to think I'm a baby, I shake my head and make myself smile. "Jojo, I was only—"

Crreeaaak!

The wooden railing falls away, crashing and banging into the darkness below. Off balance, I shriek and flap my arms. My shirt tightens against my chest and neck. Someone's pulling me back. Kerry.

I fling my arms around her. "Oh my God, you saved my life."

She clears her throat. I realize how tight my hug really

is and pull away, ears burning. Geez, can I act like more of an idiot?

"So, did you see any monsters?" Joey asks, still filming me.

I shake my head and run down the last few steps. Once at the bottom, Kerry and I shine our flashlights all around us. The smell reminds me a lot of the antiques store Mom sometimes visited back in Crescent City. Old and moldy.

"Oh, look. There's the washer and dryer." Kerry points them out with her light.

I shake my head at the dusty yellow appliances stacked with old newspapers. "Yuck. They're all rusty. Things must be fifty years old."

"You should be happy you have them," Kerry says. "When we first moved here, my mum and I had to wash our clothes at a Laundromat."

I scowl. "At least Laundromats have lights. I sure don't want to come down *here* every time I need clean socks." I think back to the pile of dirty clothes at the bottom of my closet.

Kerry giggles. "Thought you didn't mind the shadows."

"Guess I was wrong."

"Darkness is just the absence of light," Joey says matter-of-factly.

I shine my light over the shelf full of canning jars. "Yeah, but when all you see are shadows, your imagination fills in the blanks."

His eyes follow the beam. "In total darkness there are no shadows."

"Whatever." Frowning, I turn around slowly. There's a rusty old bike, over here a three-legged table. What a mess.

Kerry points her flashlight above us. "Look. That's why the lights don't work."

A cloth-covered wire snakes across the ceiling, clamped in places to thick wooden beams. It ends at a ceramic knob and an empty light socket.

"Even I know how to fix that," Joey says.

"The job is yours, little brother. You can—" As I speak, I turn to my left, earning myself a mouthful of cobwebs. "Oh, yuck." I shove the flashlight at Joey and swipe at the gunk strung across my face and shoulders.

Joey points the beam directly into my eyes. "What do they feel like?"

What does he think they feel like? I turn my back to the light. "Like cobwebs, silly!"

"Yeah, but are they thick and sticky?"

"See for yourself." I turn and drag my silk-covered hand across the front of his shirt. Joey's lips curl like I just smeared dog poop on him, and immediately, I regret my little joke.

"Stop it, Theresa." He paws at the tiny threads on his chest. "I just wanted to know if it was from a black widow."

"Black widow?" What's on my neck? My guilt vanishes at the thought of a hamster-sized creature sinking its fangs into my skin. "Get it off me!" I twirl, slapping myself all over like some freaked-out ballerina.

"Oh, stop," Kerry tells me. "There's nothing there."

Joey plucks the last strand from his shirt and rubs it between his fingers. "This silk is weak."

"So, it's probably from a daddy longlegs," Kerry says.

"Actually, daddy longlegs are not really spiders. They're more closely related to scorpions."

"What? They can sting? I didn't know that." I swing my head from side to side, trying to see over my shoulder.

"I wouldn't worry about it," he says, turning his attention to a table stacked with old magazines.

Sure, the thing's not crawling on you, is it?

Kerry tips her head to the side. "And why is that?"

"Because that web is probably from a common cellar spider," he says, running his finger across the dusty table. "Daddy longlegs don't make webs."

I quit spinning. "Okay, so are cellar spiders poisonous?" Say no. Please, say no.

He shakes his head.

I take back the flashlight. "Thanks. That's all I need to know."

Kerry aims her beam into the darkness. "Even with this flashlight I still can't see very far. This place is huge."

Yeah, huge. Big enough for all sorts of things to hide in.

Something squeaks behind us. As one, we swing our lights back toward the washing machine. Do we *see* anything move? No, but we hear it. Small. Scurrying through the darkness.

Holy crabs! "Is that what I think it is?"

"All right, so there are a few mice," Kerry says. "I suppose we should have expected it."

Expected it? We're talking about little hairy creatures, not a surprise rain shower. No matter how cute they looked in the pet shops, the thought of their little toenails clawing their way up my bare leg makes me shiver. Regretting my decision to wear shorts, I pan my beam along the floor in quick semicircles, trying to surround myself with light.

Kerry lays a calming hand on my shoulder. "Come on, Theresa. They're running because they're scared."

They're scared? I glance longingly toward the stairs and the light from the kitchen, but don't resist as Kerry nudges me deeper into the basement. There's a wall behind the washer and dryer. We step around it to discover a huge, white, rectangular box.

"Looks like a coffin for a big fat fellow," Kerry says, poking me with her elbow.

The thing really does look like a coffin.

"It's a freezer," Joey announces.

¡Tonta! Of course, it's a freezer. I step closer then stop. A brick props the top open a few inches, revealing nothing but darkness. Again, my imagination kicks in. What if there's a body in there? Or . . . something worse? I picture a Golem-like creature licking its chops at the hope of fresh meat. It's watching me now, hoping I'll heave open the lid and lean in, because then it could—

"Want to open it?"

Kerry's voice drags me back to reality, and my "What for?" comes out higher pitched than I like. Stupid. I'm too old to be acting like this. We barely take a handful of steps. An odd sound cuts through the silence, a lot like a yelp from a puppy.

It's Kerry. "I was wrong about there being mice," she mutters.

Why does she sound so disappointed? "Okay, but what made that squeaking sound?"

She aims her light at the shelves beside the freezer.

A rat the size of Dad's shoe sits up. Blinks.

"That's it. We're done." I turn and take a couple steps for the stairs. Joey is still standing there and I grab his arm and drag him with me.

Kerry hustles after us. "Hold on," she pleads. "I'm not mad about rats either, but there's only been one. We'll stay out in the open. Rats simply don't attack people for no reason. Isn't that right, Joey?"

I stop, narrow my gaze on Joey.

"That's correct," he says, peeling my fingers from his arm. "There are no known accounts of rats attacking people who are vertical and moving."

"Yeah?" Not totally convinced, I scan the floor around us. "Because I saw this old movie once, and *those* rats sure as heck—"

"This isn't a movie, Theresa." Kerry hauls me back to where we saw the rat. This time the shelf is empty. "See?" she says, giving me a big fake smile, "it was probably blinded by the flashlight."

Joey nods. "The rat was blinded . . . temporarily when its pupils contracted."

"Okay," I mumble, embarrassed for being the only one to freak out about it. "I guess I can handle one rat at a time, especially if they run off like that one did." Did I really say that? Maybe I'm braver than I thought.

The space ahead of us is a cluttered mess, just like the part we've come through. We pass all kinds of junk: a broken TV . . . boxes of old records . . . a stack of rolled up carpeting. In some places the boxes are piled as high as Kerry's head. A netting of dusty cobwebs covers most of it, giving everything a creepy, forgotten feeling.

"Joey, I hate to say it, but it looks like our grandparents were hoarders."

He nods his agreement and aims the camera in the direction of Kerry's flashlight beam. "I don't want to go that way," he announces as his nose starts to crinkle. "There's a bad smell coming from over there."

Kerry takes a few steps and stops. "Crikey, Joey's right. I think something died down here."

Died?

"Crikey." Joey repeats the word a few times as if trying it on for size.

I move closer to Kerry, and now I smell it too. "Does that mean there's a . . . a *corpse?*" Again, my voice reaches an embarrassing pitch. So much for being brave.

"Theresa . . ." Kerry smirks. "I was talking about a cat or, more likely, a rat." As she picks her way toward the mysterious odor, she raises her hand to her face. "Ugh. It's even worse over here. It's . . . it's . . ."

"Putrid?" Joey suggests.

"I couldn't have said it better myself." Kerry waves Joey over. "Come on. Like you said, I want you to document everything. Whatever it is."

"Oh, all right." With one hand holding the cell phone/camera out in front of him, he raises his free arm to his face like he's sneezing into his elbow and edges forward.

Kerry eyes a tall stack of boxes. "I can't really see what's causing the smell without pushing some of this rubbish out of the way. Do you think your dad would mind?" She pulls the neck of her tee-shirt up and perches it on her nose.

"He'll have to clean it all out anyway." With one hand holding my nose, I wave her on with my flashlight hand. "Go ahead, push."

She sets her feet. "All right, now get ready to move . . . because if there's something living in there . . ."

"Oh, wow, I didn't think of that. Hold on a sec." On a rack, a short-handled shovel hangs between a spade and some kind of pitchfork. I pull it off and position my flashlight on a stack of crates about six feet from Kerry. Breathing through my mouth, I raise the shovel over my head.

Kerry shines her light on me. "You really believe you're going to stand there and pound whatever comes at you?"

Am I? "I don't know." I take a couple of practice swings. "But holding it sure makes me feel safer."

"Okay, but watch out with that shovel, because if anything does run out, the first thing coming at you will be me." She rests her palm against the middle of the junk heap. "Ready with the camera, Joey?"

He nods.

"Okay, here goes."

She gives the pile a push and it crashes to the side, raising a small cloud of dust and destroying the homes of at least ten generations of spiders. I hear a couple of squeaks so I shift from one foot to the other, chest pounding, shovel ready. Kerry hustles toward us, coughing as she searches the floor with her light.

We only see one rat. It runs out into the open and stops, probably confused by the dust.

All pumped up, I swing the shovel and show it my teeth. "Aaaah. Get lost, you." I stomp my feet. To my relief, the thing scuttles off.

"Very impressive." Kerry grins between inhaler puffs. "Told you they would run away."

"He'd be crazy not to," Joey says. "A giant was swinging a shovel at him."

A giant? Hmm . . . never looked at it that way.

Once the dust settles, Kerry leads us back to what she uncovered, a wilted cardboard box buzzing with flies. She shines her light inside. "Aw, poor little guy."

Joey and I peek over the edge at the striped tail and hollowed out fur. It's a raccoon, or, at least what's left of one.

"Can I keep the tail?" Joey asks.

"What? No," I say, answering how I think Mom would have. "It's probably full of—Kerry, look."

I wrestle the hand she's holding the EMF meter with up to her face. Three green lights cast an eerie glow. At that moment, all three of us could win an owl eyes contest.

Kerry clutches the EMF meter to her chest. "Flipping awesome."

"N-now, let's not get too excited," I say, shining my light at the bare beams above us. "On *Ghosters* they'd check if those exposed wires on the ceiling are what's making that thing light up."

"Good idea." Kerry peers up at the spot where a cluster of old wires snake in and out of a hole. "I'll hold the EMF meter up there. If it stays lit, then it's bad wiring that's lighting it up. If it doesn't . . ." She turns to Joey. "Make sure you get this."

"Get what?"

"She wants you to keep the camera aimed at *her*," I explain. If Kerry is going to be around my brother, she'll have to be more specific.

Standing on tiptoes, Kerry raises the EMF meter up near the wires. Two of the three lights go dark, and a crooked grin crosses her lips. She heads back to the junk pile, and immediately, three lights blaze.

"That's proof," she sputters. "We've got a ghost."

"Flipping awesome," my newly British brother says. He follows my flashlight beam with the camera. "But I still don't see anything."

The little hairs on my arms stand up. Even though Kerry's device is glowing like crazy, it's still hard to accept there's a real ghost down here. With us. Now.

Kerry's holding a toy, I tell myself, failing to rub away the sudden goose bumps that have risen on my arms.

And these are popping up because I'm cold. The simplest explanation is always—

"Looklooklook." Kerry practically stuffs the EMF meter in my face. "Now we've got four lights."

Oh, man. I smile through gritted teeth. What if that thing really does work? Contest or no contest, I don't know if I'm ready to see a real ghost yet.

Joey's face glows green as he leans in to see. "What if your EMF measurer is broken?"

Kerry shakes her head. "Impossible. I just got it." She holds the glowing meter alongside her head and whispers into the camera as Joey records her. "See? Four lights. And since we can't blame the wiring that means there's *got* to be a gh—"

The EMF meter goes black. "What the . . . ?" Kerry flips it on and off, shines her light around the room. "Is that your plan? You tease us with four lights and then run off?"

As if copying the EMF meter, her flashlight goes out. "This too?" She taps it against her hand. "Blasted batteries. As much use as a chocolate teapot."

"I'm sorry," I tell her, half relieved. "We shouldn't have trusted those old—"

A dark shape explodes from the remaining pile of junk behind her.

I shriek, grab onto Kerry as she turns to see. By the time I think to aim the flashlight, it's too late.

"Whatever it was went that way," Joey says, staring into the darkness.

Kerry bounces her gaze back and forth between Joey and the shadows. "Did you see what it was?"

He shakes his head.

"Come on," I tell them. "Let's go back upstairs before *this* flashlight—"

It goes dead.

CHAPTER 7

BLACK.

Cave black.

Can't-see-your-hand-in-front-of-your-face black.

I scream. Kerry screams. Like some terrible off-key duet, we scream together.

"Joey?" I reach out for him, arms waving. God, where'd he go? Kerry calls out too. Blind, we bang into junk as well as each other.

"Come on," I say, trying to keep my voice calm. "Say something, Jojo." I move my arms back and forth in front of me. I stumble over Joey.

He lands on his back with an *ooof,* me on top of him.

"You okay?" I ask. Even though he won't like it, I feel his head, his face.

I'm not surprised to discover Joey covering his ears with his hands. Probably expects us to scream again. Even though there's a Fourth of July show going off inside me, I scramble to my feet, pulling him up with me.

"It's okay," I tell him. "We won't yell anymore."

To my relief, he doesn't shake my hand away. After a few bumps and stumbles, our eyes finally adjust, and we all work our way toward the light and pound our way up the stairs. The last one in the kitchen, I yank away the chair and bolt the door behind us.

"Oh, my gosh. That was intense."

Kerry leans against the wall. "Good thing . . . you propped . . . that door open," she pants, squeezing the words in between inhaler puffs.

It doesn't surprise me that Joey heads straight for the sink to wash up. Reminded of all the stuff I touched down in the basement, I head over too and pump three big squirts of antibacterial soap onto my hands.

"We just saw a ghost," Kerry says pushing in beside me.

"Congratulations." I offer her a soapy hand. "Guess that makes you an official ghost chaser now."

"So are you," Kerry tells me.

Laughing, we shake, then, hands dripping bubbles, turn to Joey who's heading for the refrigerator.

"You're a ghost chaser too," Kerry tells him.

"Yeah." I giggle. "Come back here so we can congratulate you."

"No thank you." He stares into the fridge. "Why are you two so happy? We don't know what that brown thing was."

He's right. It could have been anything. But if it wasn't a ghost, how do I explain the EMF meter . . . and what about the flashlights . . . ?

All the excitement has made me hungry. There's a freezer bag full of chocolate chip cookies on the table. I dry my hands on the dish towel and pull out two. One for me, one for Kerry.

She surprises me by raising her cookie high. "To our first ghost," she says, as if making a toast.

What the heck. I laugh and tap my cookie against hers. "To the ghost."

"I don't get it," Joey says, still looking into the fridge. "You're afraid of the ghosts, but you still want to find them?"

Still smiling, Kerry glances at me, then shrugs. "It sounds a bit barmy when you say it out loud, but yes—and what happened down there *was* supernatural. I mean, how else do you explain both flashlights going out at the same time?"

Joey shuts the fridge and turns toward us, a half empty jar of pickles clutched to his chest. "Coincidence," he tells her. "Those flashlights are probably as old as me. The batteries too."

I shake my head. "I had a battery-powered night light

in my room when I was little. When those batteries wore down, the light would dim little by little. These flashlights just snapped off like a switch."

Joey opens the jar and reaches in. "But we didn't *see* a ghost."

"True, but that doesn't mean it wasn't there." Kerry takes a bite of cookie and grins. "I guess the only way to make you a believer is for one to come up and grab you."

Kerry and I start to laugh, but Joey looks confused. Feeling a little guilty, I stop laughing and shake my head at Kerry, hoping she'll notice. She does. He sits down across from us, and we rest for a while, lost in our own thoughts. The only sound is the ticking of Grandma's teapot-shaped clock.

Joey finishes eating his pickle and stands up. "All I know is that something flew out of that junk pile. What exactly did you see, Theresa?"

"I don't know . . . something small. It all happened too fast, so I couldn't—"

Kerry gasps. "A ghost raccoon."

I smirk. Seriously? That's the best she can come up with?

"Why not? We all saw the body."

"Dad says there *are* no ghosts," Joey tells Kerry, "human or animal."

"O . . . M . . . G." She snatches up the phone. "What a bunch of twits. We've been sitting around here guessing and the whole time we had it recorded."

Holy crabs, she's right. I slide my chair closer to Kerry, and Joey hunches between us. The recording starts out bouncy as Joey tramps down the stairs, but once he reaches the bottom, the camera work improves. Still, it only shows what the flashlights are aimed at. We fast-forward to the part right after the dead raccoon.

"Okay," Kerry whispers, "it happens right after I check the wires with the EMF meter."

I stab my finger at the screen. "There it is."

Something brown flashes across the bottom.

I frown at Joey. "Could you have jerked the camera around anymore?"

"Probably, but what would be the point?"

With no idea how to answer, I blow out a long breath and watch the rest of the recording. After a bit, the flashlights go out, and the screen goes black. Joey covers his ears during the screaming part, which is still loud enough to make the speaker crackle. I imagine the three of us lurching through the darkness. Weird, but kind of exciting too.

Even though we can hear our voices, the screen stays black until we close in on the stairs. The phone case must have been hanging from Joey's wrist by the strap, because the recording ends with a jerky shot of his shoes and legs banging up the steps two at a time.

"So now what?" Joey asks.

Yeah, now what? I stand and push in my chair. I don't know about these guys, but I have to know what flew out of that junk pile. "We go back."

Kerry picks up her flashlight. "Look at you, the brave ghost chaser. We'll need more batteries."

I race to the drawer and pull out four more D cells.

"Those are just as old as the first ones," Joey says.

"That's true." Kerry takes two. "But we have to try. Aren't you curious to know what that brown thing was? It's probably to blame for draining those other batteries."

"I would like to know what that brown thing is, but I still think the batteries died because they were old."

Kerry shakes her head. "Remember how the EMF meter measures electromagnetic fields? That's because ghosts are made of energy. If they want to show themselves or make something move, they have to draw more energy from another source."

Joey opens the pickle jar on the counter and fishes out the last one. "Then, if a ghost drained all the flashlight batteries, why didn't it touch the one in the phone?"

Kerry squints, her mismatched eyes barely visible. "That, I can't say."

"Maybe it *wanted* to be recorded?" I suggest. Since there's nothing but juice left in the jar, I point at it, hoping Joey will get the clue and throw it away.

He doesn't. "Why would a ghost want to be recorded?" Joey asks, handing me the jar.

Kerry and I look at each other and shrug.

He munches his pickle as I empty the green liquid into the sink. "Ghosts or no ghosts, there's a good chance those batteries will die too."

Kerry flicks her flashlight on and off. "Well, they're all we've got. I suppose we'll just have to keep our fingers crossed."

"Is that supposed to preserve the batteries?" Joey's face bunches up as he examines his hands. "I don't think I can work the camera that way."

"No, Jojo, it . . ." I wave it off. "Maybe I should check in with Dad before we go down there again. He might have heard the screaming."

"I'll do it." Joey starts for the living room, pickle juice trailing across the floor.

I sprint past him. "No, that's okay. You've got a mess to clean up."

Although I really do hate sticky floors, having Joey clean up the pickle juice is really just an excuse to keep him from blabbing to Dad. It would take less than a minute for Mr. Honest to spill his guts about the broken railing, the rats, *and* the brown thing. After that, we'd not only be banned from the third floor, but the basement too.

I creep over to the living room, expecting to find Dad in front of the TV. He's not. The TV is off too. After checking the dining room and the bathroom, I hear his voice coming from the back of the house, the room he's decided to call his den. He's talking on the phone, and by the loud tone of his voice, it can only be his sister, Gloria. I head over.

"Yeah, she's fine," he tells my aunt. "She's got a new friend over right now. Joey . . . ? Well, remember how *I* got that time *we* moved . . . ? I know it wasn't a diagnosed condition back then, but . . ." There's a long pause. "Of course." His voice rises even more. "Look, I—sure, there's a risk, but what are my choices?"

Diagnosed condition? Choices? Since it's all stuff I'm probably not meant to hear, I act like I haven't and step into the room. "Is that Tita Gloria?"

Dad's sitting in front of his computer, phone pressed to his ear. Obviously surprised to see me, his eyes go wide for a moment. "Uh . . . yeah," he mumbles to both me and his sister. "Like always, she called to give me a hard time." He holds the phone up. "Say hi and bye to your aunt."

Already? I holler across the desk, "Hi and bye, Tita Gloria!"

He sets the phone down and focuses on the computer screen.

"So . . . get any writing done?" I ask.

"Just catching up on e-mail." He glances up. "Your brother all right? Thought I heard something a while back."

Joey. Right. "Yeah, that was me yelling. I kinda had some trouble . . ."

He looks up and immediately his eyes narrow on mine. "Theresa . . . ?"

"Yeah?"

"Is that cobwebs on your glasses?"

I pull them off. "Yeah, I sort of walked into some."

Even though it's probably not smart, I stick around, hoping he'll ask what I was yelling about. His eyes stay on the computer, and I blow out a frustrated breath and leave. Nobody calls me back.

Having already propped open the basement door, Kerry waits on the first step with Joey right behind, cell phone in hand.

"So? Did you tell him what happened?" Kerry asks.

"He didn't ask." I make myself smile and pick up my flashlight. Since Kerry is a step below me, our eyes are almost even. "Still think it was a raccoon ghost?" I ask.

She shines her light down into the darkness. "Let's go find out."

CHAPTER 8

WE STAND AT the bottom of the steps and hear more scuffling noises. I can't tell if the rats are running away or coming back, but they stay out of sight, so I guess it doesn't matter. We march through the laundry area and past the freezer. Kerry leads us back to the box with the dead raccoon.

I tap her shoulder. "Is the EMF meter doing anything?"

She holds it up. Nothing.

Both relieved and disappointed, I take a few steps and shine my beam into the darkness. The light reveals an open doorway. Kerry and I look at each other with stiff smiles. Joey turns on the camera.

The basement seems to be divided into three sections: laundry area, junk storage, and whatever is beyond that doorway.

"The ghost must have gone in there." Kerry starts toward it, but I grab her arm.

"Wait, what if what we saw was something real, like an animal?"

"It ran away," Joey says.

She glances at my brother and nods. "I'm going with that."

I shine my light back at the doorway. "Sure hope you guys are right." What would be worse: meeting a real ghost face to face, or some wild animal that's so freaked out it charges right at us?

We shuffle along a narrow path and shine our lights through the doorway. The area is the size of a large bedroom, and I can see two-by-fours in the few places where there aren't any cabinets. What the heck is this?

For a while, all we do is stand there. Nothing charges us, and we creep forward. Against the far wall, a workbench stretches from one side of the room to the other. Scattered across the top are what look like pieces of a tiny half assembled wooden chair. If not for the dust and all the cobwebs, a visitor might think the owner had left just a few minutes ago.

Why didn't Dad mention this place? "Hey, Joey, check it out," I whisper. "We just found Grandpa Joe's workshop."

In the center of the room stands a square worktable with a thick butcher block top. A gallon-sized can of turpentine and a can of WD-40 are the only things on it.

Kerry inches around the table. "I guess when your grandfather passed away your grandmother decided to leave this room just as he left it."

"Looks like it." I pick up the turpentine can and give it a shake. Empty. "Mom never told me much about Grandpa Joe. She sure didn't say he liked building things."

Kerry holds up the EMF meter and frowns. Still nothing.

I step toward the wall of cabinets and signal for Joey to follow.

On the other side of the worktable, Kerry stops, her light focused on the floor in front of her.

"What?" I take a few steps. "What are you looking at?"

She holds a finger to her lips and motions for us to join her. There, behind the table, is an object the size of a medium-sized dog covered by an old brown drop cloth.

Is that it? I swallow hard. It's the right size. Right color, too.

Always filming, Joey circles around to the other side.

"Pull the tarp off," I whisper. "The EMF thingy's dead, isn't it?"

Kerry nods and places her equipment on the table. "Then why don't *you* do it?" Both hands free, she gives me a push and giggles as I scurry back against the workbench. "That's what I thought."

"Ha, ha." I rub my arms, which have suddenly gone all goose pimply.

Joey notices. "Think those related to the three green lights?"

"What green lights?" My eyes flash to the EMF meter. He's right. They must have popped on while we were goofing around.

Kerry gives me a nervous smile. For a while, she just stands there, looking at the mysterious canvas-covered shape. "This is it . . . my first chance to communicate with an American spirit."

Even though my stomach feels like there's a dozen miniature cheerleaders jumping around inside it, I wave her forward. "Go ahead, Kerry. Talk to it." I light up the canvas with my flashlight. Ohmygosh! What if the thing answers?

She takes a step forward then bends at the waist, literally talking down to the thing. "Hello. I'm Kerry Addison. I'd love to speak with you."

Come on, ghost. Say something.

But it doesn't, or at least I don't hear it. From the disappointed look on her face, neither does Kerry.

She calls out a few more times and then sighs. "My gran says not to take it personally if I don't get a response. Very few ghosts are both willing and able."

"Yeah, they hardly ever hear any actual voices on Ghosters," I say, hoping to make her feel better.

The EMF stays lit, but after a few more tries, Kerry says, "All right, enough of this. Time to see what's under there." There's a broken garden rake in the corner. She grabs it, then hands me her flashlight.

"Afraid to touch it?" I ask.

She narrows her eyes on me. "Would you like the honors?"

"Maybe next time."

Spotlighted by two flashlights, Kerry grips the rake with both hands and stands as far from the canvas-covered lump as possible. "Ready, Joey?"

He nods.

"Theresa?"

I nod. For the second time in three days, an icy finger touches the base of my spine. I grip the flashlights hard, hoping to keep my hand from shaking.

Like some bored nature photographer filming his ten-thousandth deer, Joey calmly records Kerry as she hooks the tip of the rake on a tiny hole and whips the canvas onto the floor.

I gasp.

Kerry snarls. "If you guys post that on the Internet, I'll strangle you."

It's a little pink tricycle.

Instead of laughing, I lunge forward to crouch beside it. "Whoa, this is so weird."

"What?" Kerry asks. "Was it yours?"

"I think so, but I always thought I had a red one." I spin one of the pedals with my finger.

"Maybe you had two and you don't remember," Joey suggests.

"Why would I have two tricycles?"

"Does it matter?" Kerry asks. "We're looking for ghosts, remember? The EMF *and* my arm hairs say there has to be one close by."

Yeah, the ghost. I should be scared, but I can't stop staring at the trike. There's a bell attached to the right handlebar. I remember that too. Smiling, I reach down to ring it, but before my hand touches the lever . . .

Brrrrr-ching.

I jump back. It's a good thing Kerry's a lot bigger, otherwise, we'd both be on the floor.

"Did you see that?" I shout as Kerry stands me back on my feet.

"Bloody right, I did."

For a while, all we do is stare back and forth from the trike to each other. That's when we notice Joey's not filming anymore.

"Tell me you recorded the bell ringing," Kerry says.

"I recorded the bell ringing," Joey tells her, just as she asked.

Kerry grins, but since I know my brother I rephrase her question, "*Did* you record the bell ringing, Joey?"

"No."

"Arrrgh." Kerry snatches up the now lifeless meter and waves it around the room. "Hello? Ghost? Are you still here?"

It's gone. The shock of that crazy trike bell ringing has worn off, and I try to imagine what the Ghosters would do. "I think we should check the bell."

"Theresa's right." Joey says. "It could have been stuck and pulling the canvas off shook it loose."

Kerry shrugs. "I suppose that's possible."

"I'll do it," says Joey. He bends down and thumbs the little metal lever.

Brrrrr-ching, brrrrr-ching.

"It doesn't jam at all," says Kerry. "That means a ghost must have rung it." She looks at me, then Joey. "Still feeling strange?"

We shake our heads.

"I don't either," Kerry says. "It appears tonight's little adventure is over."

Already? I can see why Kerry is so into this ghost stuff. It really is a rush. I sidestep the tricycle and follow her to the door, a confused mess of relief, shock, and frustration.

"So what? You think the trike is what burst out of that junk pile earlier?"

"Well . . . yes," Kerry answers. "With the ghost's help, of course."

"But why?"

"Who knows why ghosts do what they do?" She stuffs the EMF meter into her back pocket.

Joey calls me back. "Theresa, we should look for light bulbs. You don't want to do laundry by flashlight."

Joey's right, but why does he assume it's me that's going to wash everybody's clothes? He's old enough. I leave that argument for another day, and we search the cabinets. Kerry takes the left side of the room. Joey and I take the right. Grandpa's workroom is the complete opposite of the rest of the basement. Every cabinet is neat and organized, but from what we can tell, none of them has light bulbs.

Kerry pulls out the EMF meter, frowns, then checks the time. "Seven forty-five. I should get going."

"Watch," I tell her. "One of those cabinets we haven't checked yet is going to have a huge box of light bulbs in it."

Kerry leads the way out of the workshop, followed by Joey, then me. I almost reach the door when a distant tinkling sound grabs my attention.

"Did you hear that?" I move to the far end of the workshop, the part none of us has explored yet. Again, the tiny hairs on my arms stand up. Do they know something I don't?

"What? Are the light bulbs calling you?" Kerry teases. "Theresa. We're over here. Don't leave us."

Ignoring Kerry, I yank open another cabinet. "Look what I found."

"Are there really light bulbs in there?" Kerry peeks inside. Attached to the back of the door is a tiny rack with five little hooks. A key hangs from each of them. Four have labels. The fifth, lots older and bigger than the rest, doesn't.

"I heard them," I whisper. "I was going to leave, but then I heard them."

"Like voices?" Joey asks.

I start to laugh, then realize he's serious. "No, not talking, Joey, tinkling. You know, like rattling against each other."

"Ohmygosh!" Kerry jostles me back and forth. "A ghost wanted you to find those keys."

She's right. Before the thing with the tricycle, I would have blamed the jingling on an earthquake tremor, but now I stare, heart pounding as Kerry checks the EMF meter again.

"Nothing," she tells us. "That ghost sure is a slippery thing. Rattled those keys to get your attention, then legged it."

"Legged it?" Joey asks.

"Took off." Miming a tiny runner, she points two fingers at the floor, then waggles them.

I read the tags on the four labeled keys: "Garage . . . shed . . . back door . . . truck."

Kerry points at the fifth. "You should take that one with you."

I slip the key off the hook and shine my light on it. A dark brassy color, its head is a knot of lacy metal. On the other end is a flat rectangular piece with zigzagging lines cut into it.

I squint up at Kerry. "Why take it? We don't even know what it's for."

"Exactly. None of the labeled keys are for the third floor," Kerry explains. "So there's a good chance that's what it opens. Take it."

I wince. "But I promised my dad I wouldn't go to the third floor."

With the light shining down on my hand, Kerry's face looks ghoulish. "That's okay. Having the key doesn't mean you're going to use it."

What's she up to now?

"Then why take it at all?" Joey asks, always logical.

Like a teacher dealing with two exasperating students, Kerry rests one hand on her hip. "Let's say that for some reason your dad needs to go up there. You pull out the key and say, 'Hey, Dad, look what I found.' He'll probably thank you, especially since he won't have to search this rat-infested basement to find it."

She's not fooling me. She wants to use it.

The flashlight is still shining up on her face, and I raise my chin at my creepy looking friend. "So, why keep it a secret? Why not give it straight to my dad?"

"Because then he won't . . ." She tips her head to the side, frowns. "Okay, you guessed it. I'm a ghost-obsessed idiot. But you're not. It'll be safe in your hands, but leave it right where it is, if you think that's best."

I look at Joey. "What would you do?"

"Kerry does have a point, but either way is fine."

"Whatever." I stuff the thing into my pocket.

CHAPTER 9

WE CLIMB BACK upstairs, and Kerry looks for Dad so she can thank him and say goodbye. We find him in the living room, stretched out on his recliner. He notices Kerry, pauses the TV, and sits up.

"All done chasing ghosts? Where did you guys explore?"

"The basement," I say, trying to act bored. "It was . . . interesting."

"Yeah? What did you see?"

Say it, before Joey does.

Joey opens his mouth, but I blurt out, "A dead raccoon."

Problem solved.

"And two live rats," my ridiculously honest brother volunteers.

Well, crabs. I shrug it off like I'm some junior Indiana Jones. Rats? No biggy.

Dad purses his lips. "Oh, shoot. I should have told you guys to stay out of *there* too." He looks at each of us. "But everybody's okay, right? No bites?"

"No bites," Kerry says. "The rats just scampered away."

"Good." Dad smiles at Joey. "So, did you see lots of ghosts?"

Eyebrows raised, I hold my breath. Come on, little brother. Just do what we said. Be honest, but don't volunteer anything.

He sits on the sofa and pulls one of the throw pillows onto his lap. "I can truthfully say that we did not see one ghost."

Great. Now, I can breathe.

"But there was one part I believe you should know about," Joey says.

What? I told him not to volunteer any information.

"The railing on the left side of the stairs fell off."

"Oh, gosh." Dad's gaze bounces over to me. "Theresa, that's dangerous. Why didn't you tell me?"

"Sorry." I stuff my hands in my front pockets. "It happened when we first started, and since nobody got hurt, I kind of forgot about it." Stupid, Theresa. Like he's not going to notice.

Kerry rocks from one foot to the other, obviously dying to spill the rest.

Good thing I warned her not to. Dad would just laugh and rationalize it all away. Easy to do when you aren't there to see it happen.

Before she can change her mind, the black marble clock on the mantel chimes.

"Time to go," Kerry says. "Thanks for having me over, Mr. Martinez." She turns to Joey on the sofa. "Goodbye, Joey. I had fun with you tonight."

Joey's only response is to shift his gaze from the pillow to the paused baseball game on TV.

Probably wondering why he's suddenly mad at her, Kerry flicks her gaze between me and my brother before heading for the front door.

"I'll walk you out." As I follow Kerry I make a mental note to write Joey a script for situations like that. Sometimes people expect answers, even when they're not asking questions.

I stand on the porch and watch Kerry trot down the steps to the driveway where her bike lies on its side. The sun's fallen behind the hills, but there's a headlight on the handlebars.

"Joey's not mad at you," I call down to her. "He didn't say anything because you weren't asking a question." I shrug. "It's something we're working on."

"Oh, I see. I'll try to remember that."

"Hey, why don't you come over tomorrow afternoon?" I ask. "All we need is fresh batteries."

Grinning, she picks up her bike. "I was hoping you'd say that. I'll have a few chores to do after school. Is three thirty all right?"

"Sure. And bring your torch."

"Very funny." Smiling, she waves goodbye and heads off down the gravel driveway to the street.

Once Kerry rides away, I close the door and head back to the living room. Dad and Joey are already wrapped up in the baseball game.

"Hey, Dad, can I ask you something?"

"What?" His eyes never leave the screen.

"Back at the old house . . . my tricycle. Remember the one I had when I was little?"

"Uh, yeah, I think so." He waggles his pointer finger at the TV screen. "Joey, watch this new batter. They just brought him up from the minors."

Thankfully, the guy pops out on the first pitch, so I have Dad's attention for the next few seconds.

"This probably sounds kind of dumb," I say, stepping closer, "but I always thought my trike was red. And when we were down in the basement, I found a pink one. Did I have a second tricycle here at Grandma and Grandpa's house, like for when we came to visit?"

Dad sits there for a good while, his mouth slightly open. I start to wonder if he even heard me.

He clears his throat and, with eyes glued to the next batter, says, "Uh . . . I don't know. So much time has passed since I've seen you ride a tricycle." Again, he pauses.

I wait for the pitcher to throw. Once . . . twice. The batter strikes out.

Dad winces and glances at me. "Yeah, well, I . . . uh . . . Now that I think of it, I do remember your grandparents having a pink trike here. Yeah, you . . . you rode it up and down the sidewalk when you came to visit."

"That's what I thought." I start to leave, but stop at the door. "It was good seeing my old trike down there. Reminds me of when I was little. Good times, huh?"

For a second his eyes narrow. "Yeah, good times. Now let me watch the game. And keep your brother out of that basement until I take care of those rats. I don't need him getting bitten . . . or you."

CHAPTER 10

THE NEXT DAY, Kerry comes over. I lead her into the living room and we plop down onto the sofa.

"Thanks to Joey, my dad doesn't want us going down into the basement anymore."

"No surprise there." She unzips her backpack. "I don't have to be home 'til five. Why don't we head upstairs this time?"

"Sure. I guess there's just as much chance of seeing a ghost up there as anywhere else."

"Is your dad home?"

"Actually, he's down in the basement getting rid of that dead raccoon and setting rat traps."

Kerry smiles. "Wouldn't it be funny if *he* saw a ghost?"

"Hilarious. I'd love to hear him explain that bell ringing like it did."

"I got something in the post today." After rooting around in her backpack for a while, Kerry pulls out a black plastic box the size and shape of an overfed sunglasses case. Inside is a shiny metal gadget, which she places on her open palm. "What do you think?"

"What is it?"

"It's the EVP recorder I ordered."

What? I frown at it.

"Electronic. Voice. Phenomenon?"

Ooooh, yeah. I've seen those. "Isn't that just a fancy name for a tape recorder?"

"It's not just a flipping tape recorder." She leans toward me, eyes wide. "It records sounds that we . . . the living . . . can't even hear." She places her toy on her palm like she's offering me a tiny tray of appetizers. "Brilliant, yes?"

"Yeah, brilliant, but if you don't want to catch an earful from my dad, you won't do *that* in front of him." I peer into her open backpack. "I see you brought your flashlight. I'll go get mine."

When I get back, I find Kerry's already standing at the top of the stairs.

I jog up. "Where do you want to start?"

She peeks into the nearest room, wrinkles her nose, then points down the hall. "Why don't we try the one at the end?"

"I knew it."

"What? What did I say?"

"You know. 'You should take the key,'" I say, trying to copy Kerry's accent. "'Your dad will thank you.'"

"That's the door to the third floor?" With long-legged strides she sprints toward it. "How was I supposed to know?"

"Give me a break," I mutter, racing to catch up. "We talked about it at dinner last night."

She looks the big wooden door up and down, and her lips curl into a sly smile.

"Come on, Kerry." I slide in front of her, back pressed to the door. "You heard my dad. We could crash through the floor and kill ourselves."

She jiggles the knob playfully. "Why is it that when you know you're not allowed something you want it that much more?"

I cross my arms in an effort to look tough, no easy job since she's over a foot taller. "Give it up. We're not going in."

"Don't bite my arm off. I'm just teasing. This is a big house. Your ghost probably hangs out in lots of rooms." Her eyes twinkle. "For all you know it stands over you at night when you're sleeping."

I give her a shove. "Quit that. It's bad enough knowing my house is haunted. Now I—"

Joey comes out of his room, two doors down. "What are you doing down there?"

Kerry smirks and gives me a sideways glance. "Not opening this door."

"Are you going to look for ghosts again?" He trots toward us.

Kerry holds up the EVP thingy and nods.

"My dad doesn't want us going up to the third floor," Joey says.

"Oh, you remember that too." She glances at the door between Joey's and the one leading up to the third floor, then turns to me. "All right, if you aren't willing to use that key we found, why don't we have a look at *this* room?"

Relieved, I join Kerry in front of it. "Okay, it's not like I know one room from another."

"But you were in this house before," Joey says. "When you were little."

I roll my eyes. "Aw, who remembers stuff from when they're a baby?"

"I don't know." He looks at Kerry's phone. "But can I help again? I'm done with my homework, and last night was fun."

Joey's after-school routines are practically carved in stone, so I'm surprised he's volunteering to hang out with us.

"Sure," I tell him. "Kerry's got new ghost-chasing equipment, so we could probably use some more hands."

Kerry passes Joey her phone and grabs hold of the cut glass doorknob. "Off we go."

CHAPTER 11

WITH THE DOOR closed behind us, it's like we've left one world and entered another. I click on my flashlight. Even though it's the middle of the afternoon, thick curtains block all the light, giving the room a muffled feeling.

The room is large, L-shaped. Like the rest of the house, all of the old furniture is still in place. Beside the door is a narrow table crammed with framed pictures, and I pass my light over them. Some are of strangers. Most are of Mom, but there are a few of me as a baby. With no one to stop them, spiders have taken over, tying each frame to its neighbor.

"I bet this was your gran's bedroom," Kerry whispers, glancing at the pictures as she enters.

"Looks like it." Again, no pictures of Joey. What was the deal between Mom and Grandma? Luckily, Joey's trailing Kerry, so he doesn't notice. I follow them to the far side of the room where they're checking out the big canopy bed. An old-fashioned spread the color of strawberry ice cream stretches across it.

"Want to climb on it?" Kerry asks. "Ghosters do it all the time. It might be just the thing to bring out your gran."

"No way," I blurt out. "Dad said she died in this house, probably in that bed."

Kerry shrugs. "Right, just a thought."

There are two night stands, one on each side of the bed with matching lamps. On the left, a rosary made of purple beads is draped across a foot-tall statue of the Virgin Mary. Spiders have stretched their webs from the walls to the statue and down to rectangular box in front of it. I drag my finger through the dust, snapping the web. Glossy, brown wood shines back.

I glance up at Kerry. "Want to see inside?"

She nods.

Using the same dusty finger, I raise the lid. Through the silence, a tinkling melody explodes out at me. I pull back, and the box snaps shut, cutting off the noise. Kerry's nervous laugh tells me she's as jumpy as I am.

As usual, Joey stands by, silently filming.

Again, I push the box open. This time I'm ready for the music. It tinkles away as I rummage through the contents. Earrings . . . pendants . . . bracelets. Real gold, I think.

Kerry picks up a big cocktail ring. "Look at this stuff. It's like a mini pirate chest."

I frown. "Yeah, and Mom had to know they were here, too. I wonder why she didn't take them after Grandma Carmen died."

"Maybe she didn't want them," Joey suggests.

I think of the box filled with my own mom's rings and bracelets, stowed on a shelf in my closet for when I get older. It's only been six months, and I can't count how many times I've dragged that box out just to look at them. To bring back memories.

The music slows to a crawl, and I shut the box.

"Is it getting colder in here?" Kerry asks.

"There's a thermometer on the side of the EMF meter," Joey says in his typical matter-of-fact tone.

"There *is*?" Kerry pulls the gadget from her pocket and rotates it beneath the beam of her flashlight. "Crikey, you're right. Sixty-two degrees. That's a bit cool, but it's probably because the windows are all covered up by those thick curtains. Anyway, there's still no action on the EMF."

We move around the bed. Beside the other lamp is a small cut glass perfume bottle. I give the little puffer a squeeze, and a familiar smell fills the air.

Joey's voice cuts through the darkness behind me. "Crikey, that's what we smelled a couple days ago."

Crikey? I shake my head. Not the only British expression he's picked up lately.

Kerry gasps and gives me a shove. "What? Why didn't you tell me about that?"

I shrug. "Didn't think it mattered. Joey and I were looking around, and when I opened one of the doors—I guess this one—we smelled it. Dad said it was probably left over from the real estate lady—your aunt. Supposedly, she came by and checked the place the day before we moved in. Weird that she would actually wear the same perfume as—"

"Theresa, sometimes certain smells are associated with spirit manifestation."

"When you say spirit, do you mean our grandma?" Joey asks.

Kerry nods.

Hold on. This is getting creepy. "Are you saying that when I opened that door the other day, Grandma Carmen's ghost was actually in here?"

"Could be, and with any luck, she may show up again."

Out in the light of day that would sound exciting, but not here in the dark. A sudden chill tickles the base of my spine and I hug myself.

Kerry checks the EMF meter, then holds it up for us to see.

One light. It could just be bad wiring, but what if Grandma Carmen really *is* here? The word "lurking" pops into my head even though it's probably not the type of word I should use when referring to dead grandmas. I shine my light all around. Every shadow seems sinister. I make my way through the room, half expecting to spot Grandma Carmen herself, standing patiently in some corner, waving and grinning.

> *Well, look who's finally decided to visit her old grandma now*
> *that she's been dead these seven years. Oh, do stay a while, Theresa.*
> *We'll bake cookies together.*

I squeeze my eyes shut. Stop freaking yourself out. I take a deep breath and blow it out. That's it, relax. Even if Grandma Carmen does show up, she's just your grandma . . . right? Do what the Ghosters do. Keep exploring.

I move my flashlight across the bed to what looks like a dressing table. Suddenly she's there. My grandma. Staring at me, eyes wide. Her mouth opens and a scream bursts from me. From her.

"Theresa!" Kerry shouts. "Calm down. It's just your own reflection."

"Sorry." I swallow hard and giggle at my shaking hands. Stupid mirror.

"Crikey," Joey repeats.

I get myself together and we continue exploring the shadowy sights. My light falls on a wide, wooden cabinet, even taller than Kerry. "Whoa, this is huge. It's like the one in *The Lion, the Witch, and the Wardrobe.*" I reach for the handle.

"Not so fast. Look." Kerry passes me the EMF meter. Three green lights stand out in the darkness.

Great. Again with the crazy lights. "You think there's a ghost in there?"

"We need to open it up and see."

"We? Who's we?" I hug Joey to me, but he wriggles away, filming all the while.

"Go ahead." I shove her forward. "Open it. You're the big ghost chaser."

She clips the EVP recorder onto her belt and sets her flashlight on the braided rug at our feet, freeing up her hands. "You didn't look like such a big coward back at the school library."

"There weren't any ghosts back in the school library." I wipe my sweaty hands on my pants and aim my flashlight at the cabinet, feet set, like a baseball player, ready to run at the sign of any action.

Grandma can't be in there. Why hide in a closet when she's got this big room—this whole house, for that matter?

I look at the EMF meter and gasp. "All five lights are lit, and the temperature has dropped to fifty-four." I hold up my arm. "Look, all the little hairs are standing up. I feel weird."

"Me too," Kerry whispers. "Like I'm sweaty and cold at the same time."

"So am I," Joey says, lowering the phone. "And I don't care for it."

I wave the beam around the room, and all three of us watch as it cuts through the darkness. "Anybody think there's a ghost in here?"

"You sound like you want to leave," Kerry whispers.

I crowd in against her. "Maybe."

"Hello? Is somebody there?" Kerry calls out.

Nothing moves.

I rub my arms, but the little hairs pop back up. This is even weirder than last night in the basement.

"Do you want me to open the wardrobe?" Kerry whispers.

"Geez, I don't know. I mean, you don't even know what—"

THUMP THUMP

As one, we spin around to face the cabinet, Joey pressed between me and Kerry. Since it's still closed, I stare, not sure what to do next.

Joey works his way free from our group hug and goes back to filming. "Open it," he tells Kerry, as if discussing a birthday present. "It would be interesting to find out what made that sound."

Kerry frowns at the huge wardrobe, then touches the tip of her finger to one of the handles.

Nothing happens.

She wraps her hand around it.

Nothing happens.

"Ma-maybe you shouldn't . . ." My hands tremble. "The EMF meter . . . The knocking . . ."

Kerry adjusts her feet. "Shine that flashlight over here, and get ready with the camera, Joey. I'm through mucking about."

I aim my flashlight at the wardrobe, ready to run. Even though I'm all goosepimply, a trickle of sweat drips down the side of my face.

"Go ahead," I whisper as the image of every movie ghoul I've ever seen flashes through my mind. "I'm ready."

"Okay," she whispers, "one . . . two . . . three."

CHAPTER 12

KERRY FLINGS THE doors wide.

What I don't expect is a shoebox. It falls out at our feet, spilling old photographs all over the floor.

"What the heck?" I blink, mouth open wide. "That's it?"

To my disappointment, or maybe my relief, the wardrobe is filled with the normal stuff you would expect to find in an old woman's closet, sweaters, blouses, and down at the bottom, a dozen neatly stacked shoeboxes. But the EMF meter still shows five lights. And now they aren't just glowing. They're flashing.

"It pushed that box out at us." Kerry wheezes. She grabs the EMF meter from me and checks the thermometer again. "Crikey. Forty-six degrees." Her words come out in tiny white clouds. "I'm going to try and communicate with it."

The air feels strange, not just colder, but as if the molecules are being crowded up against me. By the look on Kerry's face, I can tell she feels it. Even Joey steps a little closer to me.

Holy crabs! It's really happening.

After taking a quick squirt from her inhaler, Kerry throws back her shoulders and calls out into the darkness, "Hello? My name is Kerry."

Nothing happens.

"These are my friends, Theresa and Joey." She steps forward, away from the wardrobe. "Whoever you are, would you please make a sound? Knock, like you did before."

We wait. The room stays quiet, but I have the feeling that someone is watching me.

Kerry elbows me. "Maybe you should say something. It *is* your house."

"Think so? You're the one with the mismatched eyes." I lean toward the dresser. "Hello? Please . . . say or do something . . ."

Downstairs, the grandfather clock chimes. I flinch like somebody pulled my hair.

"Did a ghost make the clock chime?" Joey asks.

Kerry checks her watch and sighs. "No. It's supposed to ring at this hour. But hold on, I've got an idea." She turns back to the open wardrobe. "Maybe we can get the ghost to work one of the flashlights. They do it all the time on *Ghosters*."

Still feeling watched, I glance over my shoulder, then shine the light into the wardrobe. The shoeboxes cast black shadows on the back wall.

I tear my eyes away and look at Kerry. "What do you want me to do?"

Above the shoeboxes, the clothes area is divided into two sections: hanging things on the left, drawers and shelves on the right. Kerry pats a stack of folded sweaters on the top shelf.

"Set your flashlight here. Once we're out of the way, I'll ask the ghost to click it off." She turns to Joey. "And you record everything. For all we know, it could be standing in front of us and we can't even see it."

Why does she always say stuff like that? My hands tremble as I reach up to position the flashlight. I turn to leave, but Joey shoos me back with his free hand.

"Point it the other way, Theresa. The light's hitting the camera."

I nod and turn to rotate the flashlight.

Kerry mumbles something so I glance over my shoulder. "What'd you say?"

"I didn't say anything."

But I heard something. I grab my flashlight and lurch

back, aiming the beam down toward the shoeboxes. That's when I see it. Back behind the boxes. A small pale face. And is that a hand? A tiny white hand? Fear shoots through me like a garden hose filling with water. But before I can really focus, my flashlight goes out. I shriek.

"What?" Kerry shouts. "What did you see?"

Again, Joey's sandwiched between us, and we stumble back from the dresser. We bump up against the bed and I pull them to the floor.

"Down there . . ." I stab my finger at the wardrobe. "I saw . . . I saw *something*. There . . . a hand."

Kerry shines her flashlight across the room. "Are you sure?"

"Yes, I'm sure. And eyes. I saw a freaking ghost, Kerry." I jab my shaking finger at the shoeboxes, ten feet away. "It was at the bottom. In the back. A hand came out. It was small . . . and white . . . and it was trying to grab my leg."

Kerry takes her flashlight and crawls over to collect the EMF meter she'd dropped at the foot of the wardrobe. She holds it up for us to see. "It's dead now. If there was a ghost, your screams must have scared it away."

"Good." I hug Joey to me, but he squirms away and joins Kerry at the dresser. While they're busy checking behind the shoeboxes, I lean back against the bed, mind spinning. That ghost couldn't have been Grandma Carmen . . . could it? A disturbing thought pops into my head. What if it followed me over to the bed? I stare at the bottom of the bedspread, half expecting a tiny white hand to reach out from beneath it. Oh, heck no.

Sick of the dark and everything in it, I scramble to my feet and flip the light switch by the door. Just like that, my world of lurking monsters transforms into an old woman's bedroom.

Kerry gathers up the last of the photos then squints over at me. "What are you doing?"

"Who cares about old pictures?" I throw open the door. "Come on. We need to see what Joey recorded."

CHAPTER 13

WE HEAD FOR my room. Kerry calls home for permission to stay a little longer, and the three of us sit on my bed clustered around the tiny screen on the cell phone. Since the video doesn't show any ghosts, Joey goes back to his own room. But Kerry's determined to find something useful in the recording, and she makes me watch it two more times before she gives up.

"There's absolutely nothing of any value on that video," Kerry says, tossing the phone across the bed. It lands on the old pictures we've spread out between us.

It figures. I lie on my side, head propped on my hand. "Okay, so how about that new audio thingy of yours? Did *that* record anything?"

"It's possible, but I can't tell you right now. The ghost must have sucked the battery dry. I'll charge it tonight. We can listen to whatever's on there during lunch period tomorrow."

For a while, neither of us speaks, satisfied with flipping through the pictures. Then Kerry sets down the handful she's been shuffling through and looks at me, her face thoughtful. "Is Joey autistic?"

I blink. Nobody's ever asked me that, at least not without tiptoeing around the subject first. "Well, yes and no."

"What's that mean?"

I take a deep breath and do my best to repeat what I've been told. "It's not like you're autistic or you're not. It's a spectrum. That means you can have a little, or you can have a lot."

"I'm guessing Joey is closer to a little than a lot."

"Right. What he's got is called Asperger's Syndrome."

"I knew a boy back in England who had that." Her head tips to the side. "Can they cure it?"

"It's not a disease. It's a . . ." It takes me a while to remember the word. "A condition. He . . . *we* just need to work around it."

Joey. No matter what coping skills his teachers give him, he'll always be just a little bit odd. Oh, well. I guess everybody is a little odd in one way or another.

"Your dad seems to really care about him—" She backtracks. "—Not that he doesn't care about you . . ."

"Yeah, I know." I try to play it down. "It's the Asperger's. Joey needs a lot of attention; you know?" More than me, anyway.

She nods. From the look on her face I can tell she's not buying it, so I change the subject. "If we're going to do more ghost chasing, we have to figure out what to do about the batteries."

Kerry brightens. "You're right. I was just thinking about that and something else too. You probably shouldn't tell your dad about what happened in your grandma's room today."

I sit up. "What the heck, Kerry? I see a real ghost, and you want me to lie about it?"

"Not lie, just don't volunteer information. I mean, what are you going to say? 'Hey, Dad, the funniest thing happened today. We were looking in Grandma Carmen's wardrobe when some phantom creature tried to grab my leg. Oh, don't worry. I got away. All in a day's work for us ghost chasers.'"

"I see your point. If I told him that, he'd wrap me up and put me in a mental hospital." I flop back on the bed, bored with looking at pictures of people I've never met, but Kerry keeps flipping through them. "I don't get you. Those are *my* relatives. Why are you so interested?"

"Maybe there's a clue. The ghost shoved the box out at us, remember?"

Yeah, but maybe what's in it didn't really matter. Maybe it just wanted to scare us.

Kerry picks up one of the pictures and Frisbees it over to me. "There's one of you riding that pink tricycle we found."

I smile at my two-year-old self, hair pulled up in two little pigtails with the strap of my blue bathing suit sagging off my shoulder. "Aw. I'm out by the pool. I was a cute little thing, wasn't I?"

"Adorable. Hey, what happened to make your folks stop visiting your grandparents? Sounds kind of mysterious."

"I wish I knew." I reach behind me and snag Frankie, the stuffed panda bear I've had ever since I can remember. "All I know is that my mom and my grandma got into some huge fight when I was really little, and they never spoke after that. Once I even caught my mom tearing up a Christmas card my grandma sent us."

"Really? My mum argues with Nana all the time, but they always get over it."

I shrug and hug Frankie to my chest. Then this fight must have been huge, because mine never did.

CHAPTER 14

WE PICK A shady, out-of-the-way spot, far from the racket that usually goes with lunch break at a middle school. Kerry positions the EVP recorder on the picnic table between us and drops onto the bench.

"There," she announces. "We can listen while we eat."

I put down my chicken nuggets and fries and slide onto the opposite bench. A big fan of condiments, I've also brought along a handful of foil packets. I squeeze one of each onto a napkin. Mayonnaise. Mustard. Ketchup.

The EVP recording plays and Kerry's face pinches up as she watches me swirl my creation with a French fry. "You're actually going to dip your chips in that mess?"

"What chips?"

She rolls her eyes. "Sorry, I meant fries."

I offer her a big one, dripping with my peach colored blend. "It's good. Try it."

She wrinkles her nose and hunches down over the recorder, turkey sandwich in hand.

For a good while there's nothing to comment on, and we munch our food while listening to ourselves talk.

Kerry smirks. "This is weird."

"Yeah." I dip my chicken nugget. "It's like we're eavesdropping on ourselves."

From time to time somebody on the recording says something funny and we smile. When it gets to the part where we hear the two knocks, we lean closer.

"Wow," I whisper.

Kerry waves her hand. "Shh. This is where it gets interesting."

I stare down at the palm-sized recorder, and images of the scene play out in my mind.

Joey: Point it the other way, Theresa.
A sound—high pitched—almost musical, like a
stream trickling over rocks.

Kerry meets my eyes, her eyebrows halfway up her forehead. "Tell me you heard that."

I sit up straight. "Was that *giggling*?"

She plays it again.

I gasp. "It *is* giggling. But quiet . . . like it's coming from really far away."

Kerry helps me shove aside our food, and we huddle down beside the tiny speaker. Again she plays the recording back, chewing her lip the whole while.

Giggling. There's no denying it, and since none of us was laughing . . .

"Wow." As it had the day before, my skin gets all goosepimply. "That must be what I heard when I thought you'd said something."

After the fourth playback, she turns the machine off and pounds the table with both hands. "We did it. We recorded a ghost. I wonder who it could be."

Even though it's a warm day, the goose bumps are in no hurry to leave, and I rub my arms. "Well, it sure doesn't sound like my mom. I suppose it *could* be my grandmother. Grandpa Joe died there too, but it's kind of high pitched to be a man."

"Oh, I didn't know that. It sort of increases the creep factor on the house, if that's even possible."

"Yeah, but for some reason I just don't think it's either one of them." With elbows on the table, I rest my chin on my hands. "I think the recording is someone else completely. That house is over a hundred years old. For all we know, the ghost is someone else who died there . . . even way before my grandparents moved in."

I think of playing the recording for my dad, and my breath catches as I imagine his reaction.

Give it a rest, Theresa. Obviously it was coming from

the TV downstairs. Or maybe you left the radio on in your room . . .

I stand up to gather the trash from our lunches. "Kerry, *we* know we recorded a ghost's voice, but we can't prove anything."

She pulls her long legs out and over the bench and sprawls back against the picnic table, elbows resting on the sun-bleached wood. All around us kids swarm the courtyard in their little noonday clusters.

"Does it matter?"

I shake my head, but to me it does. I want to find something Dad can't laugh away.

CHAPTER 15

THE REST OF the day goes by in a blur. All I can think of is the ghost in the wardrobe and Kerry's recording. It's a surprise when Dad notices during dinner.

"Theresa?"

"Huh?"

He frowns across the table at me. "I asked if you were feeling all right."

"You've been pushing the same green bean around your plate for five minutes," Joey says.

I look down at my uneaten meatloaf. "Oh, yeah, huh."

"Are you thinking about the ghost?" Joey asks.

I remember Kerry's warning. If I don't do something fast, Joey will blab everything. "Ghost? Not me. Why? Did *you* see a ghost, Jojo?"

"No, I didn't *see* a ghost, but—"

"That sure would be something, though." I turn to Dad. "Sorry for acting weird. I was, er—thinking about my geometry class. Yeah . . . guess it, uh, has me a little worried."

He purses his lips. "Strange, you never had problems with math before. What is it you don't get?"

My brain freezes. Yeah, what? I say the first thing that pops into my head. "Circles."

"Circles?" His head tips to the side. "What, like finding their area?"

It's as good as any other lie. "Uh, yeah, area—and circumference. I . . . I keep mixing up the formulas."

"I could . . . have a look," Dad's jaw clenches as he loads his fork with mashed potatoes, "once we finish dinner."

Now that I think about it, Dad never helped me with

homework. It was always Mom. With everything, when you get right down to it.

Normally, I'd jump at the chance for a little extra attention, but since I'm lying . . . "That's okay. There's an after school tutoring group in the library. I'll check it out tomorrow."

His face relaxes. "Are you sure?"

Is that relief?

"Yeah, I'm sure." I force myself to smile. "I think what I really need is sleep."

"Sleep. That's the ticket." He gives my hand a quick pat. Then he turns to Joey, all smiles. "So, how about you, buddy? Need any help with *your* homework?"

AT EIGHT O'CLOCK, I follow Joey upstairs to bed. I've been trying to read, but my thoughts do a three-way ping pong between what happened in the basement, my dad, and what I saw in Grandma Carmen's room. No wonder I'm totally exhausted.

Since our doors are opposite each other, we pause there. Even though it's obvious that Dad likes him more than me, there's no way I can hold it against my brother. He's just Joey.

"Night, Theresa."

He turns to open his door, so I hustle over and plant a quick kiss on his cheek.

"Yuck." He turns, rubbing it off, as I expected. "What was *that* for?"

"For being you."

I WORRY MY thoughts will keep me awake for hours, bouncing around in my head like moths in a jar. Instead, I fall asleep quick and don't wake up until the alarm goes off the next morning.

Even before I open my eyes I'm already grinning. For

the first time since her death, I dreamed of Mom. We were back in our old house making chorizo sausages in the garage. I was in charge of tying the meat-filled casings into links while Mom hung the finished product up on the rack to dry. Then, as dreams tend to do, the scene changed and we were strolling side by side through the mall at Christmas time, our arms loaded with packages.

With a sigh, I climb out of bed and throw open the curtains. Back in Crescent City, it's normal to wake up to an overcast sky, but here it's already blue.

Since my relationship with Dad depresses me, I push it aside the way I always do. Instead, I spend my morning shower thinking about what happened in Grandma Carmen's room. It's obvious I've experienced a "paranormal event," as they call them on all the ghost chasing shows. But what or *who* did I see in my grandmother's closet?

I wrap a fluffy white towel around me and trot down the hall to my room. As I pull on my last pair of clean underwear, images of whatever I'd seen in the wardrobe sandwich themselves between the happy memories of my dream and considering what to wear to school today. One good thing about being the new kid: nobody knows you haven't bought any school clothes this year. It helps that I haven't grown much lately.

I pull on some shorts. When I open the closet to get my favorite red top, I sigh. There's a big pile of dirty clothes on the floor. Plus, we've barely been here a week, and already I can't find a thing. I push pants and tops aside, determined to rearrange everything by color when I get home from school. After shoving aside a few hangers, I find the top I've been looking for, slip it over my head, and turn to leave.

My mother is sitting on the bed. Dressed in the same white capris and tee-shirt she was wearing the day that teenager smashed into her car.

"Mommy?" My damp skin chills.

Looking very much alive, my mother stands and opens her arms wide the way she's done a thousand times. In my head, joy and dread crash into each other like bumper cars. But the need to touch her wins out, and I throw my arms around her.

"Mommy, what are you doing here? Everybody said you were dead."

She takes my hand, and without a word, we climb onto the bed and sit cross-legged, facing each other.

She leans toward me, our foreheads almost touching. "I was wrong, baby. There's something you should know."

I wipe my eyes with the heel of my hand. "What?"

"Take this." Her voice cracks as she sticks out her hand, palm up.

It's a key.

I gasp. "What's it for?"

She presses it into my palm. "It's going to be scary, but you have to look anyway."

Pulse racing, I frown. "I don't understand. Mommy—"

"You need to know, Theresa. Look."

Look? I stare down at my hand. Okay, so it's a key. A really old key. Still not sure what she expects, I look up.

She's gone. In her place is a shiny black box. Small. Shoebox sized. I jump off the bed. What is going on? "Mom?" I throw open the bedroom door and peer up and down the hallway. "Mom?"

No answer.

This is crazy. I step back inside and close the door.

The box is still sitting on the bed. But it isn't shiny anymore. Now, it's soggy and warped with a rusty metal padlock. I look at the key in my hand. Why not? She said I should look.

For such a small box, it's really heavy, but I manage to drag it toward me across the bed and slide the key into the lock. Slowly, the parts click and clack into place.

I raise the lid. What the heck . . . ?

Water spills from the box, onto the bed, the floor, drenching the carpet. I leap to the floor, not sure what to do. My lime green bed skirt is already soaked six inches up. In seconds, my knees are wet. Shoes and books float past, bumping against my thighs.

I shout at the empty room, "Mom!" Nothing. "Mom . . . where are you?"

Then I hear her voice. "I was wrong, baby. It'll be scary, but you need to know. Look."

"Look?" I pound my fists into the water, head throbbing. "I did look." I slosh my way back to the door. Locked.

I have to get out of here.

The window.

I could open it; let the water spill out into the yard. Hopeful, I turn.

Holy crabs, it's gone.

The window I peered out just a few minutes before is replaced by a blank wall.

I shiver as the icy water reaches my chest. All of the stuffed animals from my bed are floating now, along with my hair brush, the shoebox full of photographs, and the three little bottles of nail polish I keep on the dresser.

I should climb up on the bed. It's my only chance. I raise my foot, trying to pull myself up. But no. Like stepping in pudding, my feet sink into the mattress.

Sobbing, I slap the water with my arms. Anger, frustration, fear, they all burst from me as tears, mixing with the ever-rising lake that surrounds me.

All this time, the water never stops flowing from the box as it bobs alongside my shoes and soggy paperbacks. Even my unicorn poster isn't safe. Something bumps against my ankle. I peer through the water and gasp. It's me. Lying on the floor. Staring up. Dark hair swirling.

"Help!" My screams echo off the walls and I tip my head back. In no time the water reaches my mouth. I pinch it shut to avoid swallowing. But that's only putting off the inevitable, because already the water—

CHAPTER 16

BEEP BEEP BEEP

My eyes fly open. Gasping and coughing, I turn off the alarm with one quick smack, then clutch at my bedcovers. They're dry. Oh, thank God!

Once I catch my breath, I scoot to the edge of the bed and check out the rug. It's dry too. I sit up, blankets hugged to my chest. It was all just a dream—no, more like a nightmare. My eyes narrow and I scan the room.

That box. That stinking, little box. If I see it, I'm going to run away fast enough to leave a cartoon cutout of me in the door. Thankfully, everything seems to be in its place. I let out a loud sigh and collapse back on my pillow, eyes closed. What a freaky dream.

But I've got to get ready for school, so I throw back the covers and start for the bathroom to take my morning shower. Just what I need. More water.

I DO FEEL better after the shower, but it doesn't help that I'm wrapped in the same white towel from the dream.

Well, unless I plan on going to school in my pajamas, I have to go back to my room. But what if Mom's there, sitting on the bed when I open the door? In the dream we hugged, but this is real life. I'm not so sure if I can hug a dead person, even if she is my own mother. I adjust my towel and glance up at the damp bathroom ceiling.

"I love you, Mommy, but please don't put me through that." I swab a face-sized circle in the steamed up mirror and stare into my own eyes, large, green, and so much like hers. Do crazy people know when they're crazy?

"Well, I can't stay in here forever." I crack open the

bathroom door and peek down the hall. All nine doors are shut, so I tiptoe down to my room and yank open the one to my bedroom.

There's nobody there. Still, the idea of Mom's ghost popping out at any second makes my stomach twitch. I look over my shoulder twice on my way to the dresser, then tug on the first shorts I find in the drawer. When the time comes to pull on a top, I gather it up in my hands first so my eyes will be covered for the least possible amount of time. A deep breath and I tug the shirt down over my head and look at the bed. The only one staring back is Frankie, my stuffed panda.

There's a framed picture of Mom on the dresser. I pick it up and slide my finger across her one-inch face. "I love you, Mommy, but I don't think I could handle finding you in my room. You understand, don't you?"

After some sloppy bed making I leave the room with an equal mixture of relief and shame. Like every other weekday, Dad has already taken Joey to school, but strangely, I'm not scared. It's like the place feels empty, not just of people but of ghosts too. I trot downstairs for the same breakfast I eat every day, a bowl of granola topped with sliced grapes. As I chew, my mind turns to the box of old pictures that fell out of the wardrobe. They were in the dream too. All those faces. Grandma's friends. Her relatives back in Spain. Mom would know at least some of them, but I sure don't. Then I remember that I was in the dream too. Floating under the water.

My breakfast becomes an icy lump in my stomach. Try thinking of something else.

I dump out what's left of it and leave my bowl and spoon in the sink to wash when I come home from school.

Think of what you'd do if you won the contest. I tell myself. The kitchen could sure use some remodeling. Who doesn't have a dishwasher? I can live with the antique stove, but the refrigerator belongs in a museum along with the screwed-up toilets and the claw-foot bathtub with the leaky shower curtain. Don't forget the busted air conditioning. I sigh and jog back upstairs to brush my teeth and gather my books for school. No wonder Dad gets mad when I suggest fixing the pool for Joey. I sure hope we win that *Ghosters* contest. Then we'll have more than enough money to fix that stuff. Maybe Dad will hug me then.

I GET TO school and find Kerry sitting alone on the low brick bench in front of the school flagpole. The first thing I do is spill my guts about the dream.

She shakes her head. "And I thought mine were strange. Yours is award-winning."

"No kidding. It was bad enough having the dream, but now I feel guilty."

"Why should you feel guilty?"

"Because when I stepped back into my bedroom this morning and didn't see her, I was relieved." Tears fill my eyes. "I didn't *want* to see her, Kerry."

"I'm sure your mum would understand. Does *any* of that dream make sense to you?"

I throw up my hands. "No, and I've gone over it a thousand times. She said she wanted me to *see*. See *what*, a box full of water? I don't understand. Why did she put me through that? She died from a car crash, not drowning."

Kerry puts her arm around my shoulder and gives me a shake. "Dreams are weird. They don't always have to mean something." She dips her head to look me in the eye. "But if your mum was sending you a message . . ."

"What? To never go swimming? Or are you talking about the third floor again? Don't even go there, Kerry." Since Frankie the Stuffed Panda is sitting back home on my bed, I hug my backpack. "Maybe I should just be happy I got to see her again. The dream really was nice . . . at least the first part."

"In the dream, your mom gave you a key. Did it look like the one we found down in the basement?"

Maybe it did, but the last thing I need is Kerry knowing. I shrug.

"That's the second key a ghost has given you." A smile touches her lips. "You've got to admit that's a bizarre coincidence."

"Are you using my dream as an excuse to ignore my father's orders? Why would my mom want me to go up there anyway? From what Dad says, the third floor's been locked up tight for like fifty years. I doubt if Mom ever went up there herself."

"That might be true, but as a ghost, she may know something that she didn't know when she was alive. Have you ever had a dream anywhere near as odd as this one?"

"No, and I've never *ever* dreamed about my mom before." My shoulders sag. "I'm confused. If you're right, my mom wants me to do something that my dad doesn't want me to do."

"I noticed that too, and—"

The annoyingly shrill buzz of the school bell cuts through the air.

She jumps up. "Oh, well, time for class. And don't worry. We'll sort things out."

"Oh, sure. As long as sorting things out means using that key." I stand, banging my shoulder into her on purpose.

She wobbles a few sideways steps and smiles. "Well, whatever you do, just make sure I'm there with you."

CHAPTER 17

AFTER DINNER, I go up to my room to work on my science report, but the dream keeps creeping back into my thoughts. Science is fun when there's an experiment to do, unlike this assignment.

Tonight, I have to read a twenty-page story about Sir Isaac Newton. Ugh. I'd rather read about the guy who invented Fig Newtons. Sure, Sir Isaac discovered gravity and all, but the man's been dead for hundreds of years.

Ready for a break, I get up from my desk and raise my arms to stretch as I tour the room. In the dream, my paperbacks were floating in the water. I half expect them to be all swollen and water-warped, but there they are, lined up on their shelf, as skinny straight as they should be. Frankie, the bear is in his place too, snuggled up on the bed beside my three-foot-tall giraffe, Gerald. I saunter over to the dresser and flip open the green-stained glass box my mom made me less than a year ago. Inside are a dozen randomly shaped bits of pink-and-orange stained glass, the pieces for the light catcher Mom and I will never finish. On top of it all sits the key I pocketed down in the basement. It stares up at me, all quiet and innocent. I pick it up and trace the notched edge with my finger. It's heavy for something so small. I close my fist over it. Should I tell Dad I have it? Why? I don't even know what the thing opens.

The big green numbers on my clock radio tell me it's 7:45. At eight, Dad will come up to say good night to Joey. That's more than enough time to see if the key works.

As I'm thinking, my feet carry me to the bedroom door. I throw it open. There's a light switch just outside, but I don't need to flick it. The night light Joey told Kerry about is plugged into a wall socket a few feet down the hall. Not enough light to read by, but plenty to get me to the bathroom without killing myself. At the far end of the hall, the back stairs are totally dark. But I can still make out the door to the third floor a few feet to the right of them. It stands out in the gloom, teasing me. I open my fist and look at the key. Like tiny teeth marks, red notches mark my skin. And I was worried about Kerry pushing me into it.

Across the way, Joey's video games blare on behind his closed door. To my left is the main staircase. There's no sign of my dad, but I tiptoe over anyway and have a peek. Satisfied that he isn't coming, I shuffle back in the opposite direction.

All I want is to find out if I've got the right key. After that, I'll definitely go back and finish reading that stupid story. I draw in a deep breath and blow it out slowly. So, if I'm not doing anything wrong, why am I acting so sneaky?

Once I pass Grandma Carmen's room, I make a slight left and stand in the shadows at the top of the servants' stairs, listening. If Dad's in the kitchen, I'll hear him. From what I can tell, he's still watching TV.

"Stop fooling around and do it," I mutter under my breath.

The door leading to the third floor is just to the right of the stairs. Again, I feel a flash of sadness when I stand in front of it. Weird, since the thing's no different from all the others doors on this floor. As it did before, the feeling disappears as quickly as it came, and I slide the key into the lock. It doesn't turn. I chuckle. What a joke. After all that drama, it's not even the right one. I start to pull it out, but stop. Somehow I know. It *is* the right key.

After a bit of jiggling, the lock gives some, but it still needs help. And what do you do with a rusty lock? Spray some WD-40 into it. I know I've seen a can somewhere in the house. Oh, yeah, down in the basement. Perfect.

I flick the light switch by the servants' stairs and take the steps two at a time, blasting into the kitchen, a girl on a mission. I know just where to find the spray can. It's on top of the butcher-block table back in grandpa's workshop. All I have to do is run down there, grab the can, and run like heck back up the stairs. The trip shouldn't take more than a minute or two, tops.

I slide the bolt on the basement door and try the light switch. Nothing. Why doesn't this switch work? Dad said he replaced the stupid light bulb down there. Then I remember him mentioning something about a fuse box and not having the money to pay for an electrician. Figures.

After propping the door open with a chair, I grab one of the flashlights from the drawer. At least Dad replaced the old batteries with rechargeables. I turn toward the open door and freeze at the sight of the cave-like opening. Am I really going down there? By myself? What if the ghost is strong enough to push the chair out of the way?

I lug over another one and position it next to the first. "Try shutting that," I mutter and click on the flashlight. With a deep breath, the kind a person might take before jumping off a sinking ship, I head down the stairs. "Relax. This'll be easy."

Dad set rat traps, but who knows if they've worked? In my hike down the stairs I imagine rats migrating across the basement floor like a herd of tiny buffalo. But I get to the bottom and the floor is empty. Good.

"I'm back," I call out, announcing myself to my furry hidden audience. "The big bad giant is back. Run. Hide. I'll only be down here for a few seconds anyway. Then you can get right back to eating dead raccoons, or whatever it is you guys do for fun."

Knowing the layout of the basement gives me some confidence, and I glide around the stacks, making my way back to Grandpa's workshop. There's the table, and there's the spray can. Yellow and blue, red cap. I give it a shake. Almost full, too. Everything's going as planned.

Yeah? So, where's the tricycle?

When we left the basement the other night, the trike was

right there beside the worktable. I pan the light all across the floor. Did Dad move it? Goose bumps rise on my arms.

Who cares? I've got what I came for. I aim my flashlight toward the exit and gasp.

CHAPTER 18

THE TRICYCLE IS blocking the door to the workshop.

Its handlebars glisten harmlessly as the beam of my flashlight slides across them. Just an old pink tricycle with a cute little bell.

Yeah, but who moved it across the doorway? It's blocking my way out.

Sweat beads pop out all over my skin, and I shiver.

"Listen up," I tell the ghost, not feeling nearly as brave as I try to sound. "You really have a thing about that tricycle, don't you? I don't get why, but I promise I'll try and figure it out." I take a step forward. "Well . . . gotta go." With long determined strides, I step up to the tricycle and pick it up by the handlebar.

Brrrrr-ching.

If the tricycle magically turned into a rattlesnake, I would not have dropped it any faster. I don't even see the thing hit the ground because the flashlight goes out as I open my hand.

Everything goes black. No workroom. No tricycle. Just the sound of my own shaky breathing. Totally freaked, I throw myself forward, a terrible move since the trike is right there in front of me. I stumble over it, and to avoid a face plant, drop the spray can as well as the useless flashlight.

Trike or no trike, I'm not leaving without that can. I scramble, claw the dirt floor. Of course, I find the flashlight first.

After breaking two fingernails, I finally locate the can, and like a blind toddler, crawl toward where I *think* the door is, one cautious hand stretched out in front of me. My fingers touch the trike's front wheel and I pull back like I'm burnt. That darned tricycle is still blocking my path, flipped on its side like some wounded animal. I stand and kick the thing away. My hands finally grip the door frame, and I breathe a little easier. From there I can make out a hint of light from upstairs. Instinct tells me to run, but I force myself to shuffle toward it, arms waving in front of me so I don't crash into something. After what seems like forever, I can see the stairs well enough and I sprint up them, half blind with tears.

Back in the kitchen, the time on Grandma's teapot-shaped clock blows me away. Less than five minutes have gone by. Still plenty of time before Dad heads upstairs. For now he's still in the living room watching his baseball. I hear the announcers going on about some rookie third baseman the Giants just signed.

Slow down, I tell myself. First, you have to put the chairs back. Once I do, I look myself over. My pants are dirty, but at least they haven't ripped. Since I really don't want to explain why I'm standing in the middle of the kitchen with dirty knees and hands, I toss the flashlight in the drawer and race up the back stairs, WD-40 in hand.

Crazy ghost. Why did it trip me up like that? All I want to do is open that stupid door. I frown up at the hallway ceiling. Geez, Mom, I love you and all, but why couldn't you be more specific about what you want me to look at?

I reach the top of the stairs and stop in my tracks. What if that ghost was Grandma Carmen? Is she on Dad's side, protecting me from harm? Well, I don't care. After all I've been through, that door is going to open.

I peer down the main hallway. With no sign of Dad or Joey, I walk the few steps to the mysterious door. The key is still in the lock. Dumb move. What if Joey saw it?

I pull the key out, squirt the hole a couple times, and then jam the key back in. After a few jiggles, the lock swivels a half turn and clicks. It works. Adrenaline floods through me. I set the can down and peek inside. Nothing. It's too dark.

Okay, I've got the right key. This should be where I head back to my room for some more Isaac Newton. So why is my hand still holding the knob? If I go in there I'll be breaking all kinds of promises. To Dad, to Kerry, and even myself. And why risk it when Dad will be up any minute?

I imagine my father's voice: Curiosity killed the cat, Theresa.

Yeah, but satisfaction brought him back.

With shaking hands, I shove the key deep into my pocket. The door lets loose a loud creak when I push it open.

There's a small landing about four feet square. I shuffle inside, leaving the door open for light. On the other side of the landing is a steep staircase, blocked by what seems like the life's work of a hundred spiders.

I sigh. Great, more spiders.

But what's at the top of the stairs? The light from the hallway only reaches the bottom couple of steps. I remember seeing a light switch outside the door. But there's no time for that now. Dad will be on his way up soon. Before I can turn to leave, the shaft of light narrows then disappears altogether. I swing around just as the door clicks shut behind me.

CHAPTER 19

FOR THE SECOND time tonight, I see nothing but black. I feel for the knob, but just like before, it won't budge. Fear presses me to the door. "Come on, you stupid door, open."

Again, I jerk the knob from side to side, but the lock refuses to cooperate. Of course the spray can is on the other side.

Knowing Dad will kill me if he finds me here, I do my best to rattle the door off its hinges. Holy crabs! Something could be creeping down those stairs right now. I peer over my shoulder into the darkness. If even one of those steps creaks . . .

I jerk the knob for the hundredth time, and to my relief, the parts that were stuck fall into place, and the door snicks open.

Thank God. I sure don't want to explain to Dad why I'm—Something slides across my bare ankle.

With a shriek, I bang my way out into the hall and grab the door, ready to slam it shut. No, don't. I tell myself. You've made more than enough noise already.

Breathing hard, I close the door quietly and turn, ready to sprint back to my room. That's when I hear footsteps coming up the main staircase. Oh, no. Dad's early. There's no way I can make it back to my room without him seeing me.

But the servants' stairs are right there, a few feet to my right. I turn off the light there and scurry down them just as Dad reaches the top of the main staircase at the opposite end of the hall.

From the shadows, I squat down and peer between the

banister railings as he pads down the hall toward Joey's room. The blank look on his face tells me I've hidden myself in time.

He stops at Joey's door. But he doesn't knock. Instead, he stares down the hall at the door to the third floor. OMG, did I leave the key in the lock? I pat my pocket and breathe a little easier when I feel the lump. Okay, Dad. Knock on Joey's door and head on inside so I can—Oh, no!

For some reason, he heads down the hall in my direction. With the lights off in the kitchen, the stairs are a black well behind me. Sick of running around in the dark, I hold my breath as my heart tries to burst its way out of my chest.

But instead of turning toward me and the stairs when he gets to the end of the hall, Dad stops to study the door to the third floor. Hands clenched, his lips are pressed in a hard line. Why? He knows the door is locked. A strangely posed statue, I crouch in the shadows, a silent witness. Too bad my left foot is going to sleep.

Oblivious to his little audience, Dad rubs his palm along the tall wooden door like he's comforting an old friend. Then, for a few moments, he just stands there, head bowed. When his lips start to move, I press my forehead to the railing. Darn it, I can't hear a thing. Pins and needles creep up my calf. I absently rub it, eyes never leaving my Dad.

Finally, he turns and heads back the way he came.

Good, now go inside Joey's room. Numb from the knee down, I shift my weight, and the stair riser creaks beneath me. Doggonit! Like some automatic defense system, my eye flood with tears as I grab the railing and pull myself to my feet.

Dad spins around just as I to climb the last few steps. He comes at me . . . fast. Grabbing my shoulder, he yanks me toward him. "What were you doing there?"

"Nothing . . ." I blubber. "I was just coming upstairs. Honest."

"In the dark?"

Somewhere down the hall, a door opens.

"Dad, what are you doing to Theresa?" Joey stands in the middle of the hallway dressed in nothing but his underwear and a tee-shirt.

"We're just talking, Joey, it's . . . it's okay . . ." Dad lets go, but his eyes still hold me. "You weren't watching me?"

"No, I-I just got here. Why? Is something wrong?"

His eyes narrow. "Don't worry about it." He turns back to Joey, a big fake grin is pasted across his face. "Just a little misunderstanding, Jojo. No big deal."

A little misunderstanding? I rub the spot where his hand gripped my arm. Since he doesn't seem to want to kill me anymore, I sidestep past him, more than ready to get back to my room.

"Theresa . . . ?" Dad rakes his fingers through his hair. "I'm sorry I acted so crazy. You just surprised me is all."

"That's okay. I should have said something."

"What were you doing down there, anyway?"

All of a sudden the rug is really interesting. "I, uh . . . I was in the kitchen . . . looking for a snack."

He looks at my empty hands.

I shrug. "Nothing looked good." Wow. That lie sure came easy. Guilt nibbles at my brain. I stuff my hands into my pockets and study the carpet some more.

"I'm going to bed," Joey announces. His room is across from mine, and we follow him back.

Dad looks at me sideways, obviously still suspicious. "Maybe you should go to bed too."

At that moment, I'm relieved to do just that.

CHAPTER 20

AT LUNCHTIME THE next day, Kerry and I make our way to our usual table at the far end of the school's courtyard. She listens, a lopsided grin on her face, as I tell her about last night's adventures.

"Crikey, every day it's something. I warned you not to go looking for ghosts without me."

"I wasn't looking for ghosts. I was looking for the WD-40 can so I could get the lock open."

She slides onto the bench. "I bet you'll think twice before you go down into the basement by yourself again."

"You got that right." I drop into my spot across from Kerry and start to unwrap my taco.

"Do you have any idea why the ghost wanted to block you from leaving your grandfather's workshop?" she asks.

"None."

"There could be more than one ghost, you know."

Never thought of that. "That's true," I mumble through a mouthful of taco. "One that wants me to see the third floor . . ."

"And another one trying to stop you. I mean, why else block your way with the tricycle?"

For a while we eat in silence. Around us kids eat their lunches too, most likely chatting about normal things like boyfriends or what they watched on TV last night.

Kerry stretches her arms wide. "How many of them do you think have ever seen a real ghost?"

"Probably none." I take a sip of milk. "Do you still want to come over this afternoon? It's Wednesday. We can watch *Ghosters*."

She grins. "Got any more chocolate chip cookies?"

THE MOMENT KERRY steps into the living room her shoulders droop. "I thought we were going to have chocolate chip."

"Sorry, all out of chips. These are snickerdoodles." I pick up the plate from the coffee table and turn like I'm heading back to the kitchen. "Okay, if you don't want them . . ."

"No, no, no. I'm sure they're great." She grabs two.

That's what I thought. I smile and set the plate back on the coffee table.

Kerry flops onto the sofa. "Where is everybody?"

"Upstairs. Dad's taking a nap and Joey's doing his homework."

"Well, turn the TV on. *Ghosters* is going to start any minute, and I don't want to miss the theme song."

Soon we're both giggling as we try to hum along with the opening music, but as the show gets going, we realize what experts we've become.

"We had a lot cooler stuff happen to us," Kerry grumbles. "Last year's winning video was just a creepy shadow on the wall."

"Too bad Joey couldn't record that ghost I saw in the wardrobe." I lean forward, eyes glued to the screen. Tyson O'Seanesey and Billy Joe Francisco, the stars of the show, are creeping down a stone staircase somewhere beneath a two-hundred-year-old church.

"We got the giggle on tape," Kerry reminds me.

"I know, but we can't prove it's a real ghost. It's not like we can compare it to some database."

"What if there really was a database?" Kerry holds her hand to her ear as if she's talking into a phone. "Hello, Miss Martinez? Good news. We checked your giggle against our G.G.D. That's the Ghostly Giggle Database. And we have verified your giggle did indeed come from a ghost. Oh, you're quite welcome. Have a lovely day." She hangs up her imaginary phone and sits back, flashing a huge smile.

"You're hilarious." I grab a pillow and smack her in the face.

"Hey! At least we actually *have* a ghost."

"All right, but what good is that if we can't prove it?"

"Well, it's not as though the ghost is going anywhere. It'll probably be here longer than you. Relax. Watch the show."

During the commercial break, they play an announcement we've both heard a thousand times.

> *There is still time to enter the Third Annual* Ghosters *Contest. Submit a recording of your paranormal experience by October 1st. Three finalists will be selected. First, second, and third place winners will be judged on the* Ghosters' *own experiences when they visit each of the three locations. Hurry, because your submission could win you up to two hundred thousand dollars! Winners will be announced on October 31st on a special Halloween edition of* Ghosters.

Dad sure would love having all that money. I imagine him throwing his arms around me when I hand him one of those giant-sized checks. Sweet.

Kerry stands up. "We can still win that contest."

"You really think so?" I rest my socked feet on the coffee table.

She bends over me, hands on hips. "Theresa . . . are there ghosts in this house?"

As if on cue, the TV remote slides across the coffee table.

I pull my feet up onto the sofa. "Well . . . yeah, obviously."

Kerry grabs the remote and waves it at me. "See? It *wants* to be recorded. We'll get something eventually, and when we do, it will be loads better than that stupid shadow figure from last year."

Pumped, I hop up on the sofa to look her in the eye. "You're right. We *can* win." I start bouncing. "We *will* win.

And with all that money Dad can get the house painted. We can get this whole place remodeled."

Kerry joins me, and we hold hands as Grandma Carmen's cushions spill onto the floor with each hop. "I'll be able to buy all the ghost chasing equipment I want." She grins. "All we have to do is get up to that third floor, and . . ."

I stop jumping and flop down onto the sofa.

"What?" She drops down beside me.

"*You* know what. You're on that third floor kick again."

"Well, why not? You had that dream. *And* the ghost locked you in there. *And* it touched your ankle. There's something up there you need to see."

"Oh, come on," I say in a tiny voice that's almost a sob. "Last night my dad went nuts when I wasn't even *touching* that door. What do you think he'll do if he catches us up there? Plus, there's that other ghost . . . the one that blocked my way with the trike."

"Ugh. Forgot all about that." Kerry sighs and stretches out on the sofa, eyes on the ceiling. "My uncle Scott came over last night."

I stare out the window. "Awesome, is he a ghost who wants us to film him?"

"No, he's Aunt Amelia's husband . . . *and* he's not dead. I told him and my folks all about what we've been doing."

"And what did they think?"

"Uncle Scott was really interested. He even offered to lend me his video camera."

Oh, the ghost-chasing uncle. "Why loan you another video camera? You already have one in your phone."

"Not like this one. It's full spectrum. You can see in the dark with it."

I sit up and start piling the throw pillows back on the sofa. "That sounds expensive."

"It is. The only reason he's loaning it to me is that he's buying an even better one. He's kind of obsessed."

More than you? I try not to smile. "Is he in some kind of ghost chasing club?"

"Yeah, they travel around the country exploring creepy old buildings. Like your house." She winks and sits up. "You know, if you tell your dad about the contest, he might change his mind about letting us explore up there."

I stand and gather up the rest of the scattered cushions. "Maybe, but don't get your hopes up. From the way he was acting last night, there's something he isn't telling me about the third floor. Anyway, even if I do bring up the contest, he'll probably say it's a stupid waste of time."

As I bend to pick up a cushion next to Kerry's foot, and she grabs my arm and pulls me onto the sofa. "You mean, like *you* were with that key?"

"Yeah," I nail her full on with a green satin cushion, "like I was with the key."

"Hey! No fair." She throws the pillow back, but I'm already blocking.

The battle continues off and on through the rest of the show.

When it's all over they play the contest announcement one more time. Kerry stands and glances at the staircase. "Time to go. Shame we can't see what's up there." She takes a few steps toward the front door and turns back. "Hey, what do you think about me spending the night on Saturday? I'll bring the new camera."

"Sure. There's no reason the ghosts won't be haunting some other part of the house."

CHAPTER 21

THE DOORBELL RINGS on Saturday evening, and I peer down the main staircase to find Dad has already opened the front door. I hang back and watch from the hallway upstairs.

"I think Theresa's in the kitchen." Dad tips his chin toward Kerry's backpack, which is so stuffed, it looks like the zipper's going to bust. "That looks heavy. Want me to take it upstairs for you?"

Kerry blushes as she shrugs out of her purple sweat jacket. "That's all right. I can do it."

"What? You think going up and down those stairs is going to wear this old guy out?" he grumbles, making his voice sound old and scratchy. "Jumping Jehoshaphat. I'm not that old."

Kerry's brow crinkles as she watches him limp dramatically back into the living room. "I-I didn't mean you were old, Mister Martinez."

Why doesn't he do stuff like that with me?

Dad spins back around. "Sorry, Kerry, I was just messing with you. Go ahead. Take it up yourself." He waves his arm in the direction of the stairs.

Kerry heads up the stairs, looking a little confused, and I dash back to my room to hide in the closet. I wait, door slightly open, and spy on Kerry as she steps into the room. She sets her backpack on the chaise longue in the corner and stands there a few moments, just looking around. I'm about to jump out.

"Hello?" No answer. "Hello. My name is Kerry. Is anyone here?"

How can I pass this up? I cup my hands to my mouth and in my best ghostly voice call out, "Helloooooooo."

She shrieks and spins around, her eyes like golf balls. "Crikey, Theresa, I almost wet my knickers."

I laugh. "Sorry, I couldn't resist. Come on downstairs and see what we're having for dinner this time."

She sets her pack down and clutches her chest. "Hold on. I have to shove my heart back down my throat." After a few deep breaths she starts for the door.

I grin. "Well *that's* rude."

She turns around. "What is?"

"You haven't said goodbye to the ghost."

SINCE KERRY ASKED for Mexican food the last time, I've decided to make enchiladas, an easy recipe that Mom had made more than once. Again, she helps with the salad. As I'm stirring the red sauce, I ask, "Did you bring that camera your uncle loaned you?"

She looks up from slicing cucumbers. "Yeah, and it's really cool, too."

"Why don't you bring it down so I can see it?"

"Your dad won't mind?"

"Naaah, not if we stay here in the kitchen. Go get it."

Hardly a minute passes when Kerry clomps back down the servants' stairs and into the kitchen. But instead of the camera, she's carrying my red spiral notebook. With a goofy grin, she grabs my arm, yanking the spoon away in mid-stir.

"What's wrong with you?" I ask, blinking at the red spray of sauce across the floor.

She holds up the notebook. "Does this mean what I think it means?"

"What? My science notes? Yes, Sir Isaac Newton hated apples."

"No, silly. That you've decided to explore the third floor."

I back away from my crazy friend and tear off a handful of paper towels. "What are you talking about?"

"*This*," she holds up the key to the third floor, "was

sitting on top of *this*." She waggles the notebook in front of my face.

"Huh?"

The notebook is folded open, and she holds it steady for me to read. The page is blank except for one word written in shaky blue letters, two inches tall: *LOOK*.

The spoon falls from my hand, splattering more sauce across the linoleum. "I-I didn't write that."

"What? I thought . . ." Kerry looks from the key, to the paper, then back at me. "They were sitting right there in the middle of your desk."

I hold my finger to my lips and run down the hall to check on my dad. Satisfied that he's still parked in front of his flat screen, I race back into the kitchen. Kerry's already pulled her inhaler from her back pocket. She's barely finished breathing in her asthma medicine as I grab her arms.

"It was the ghost," I squeal.

"Obviously, it wants you to go up there."

"Wait." I stare up at Kerry, eyes narrowed. "This isn't a trick to get back at me for pranking you upstairs, is it?"

She shakes her head hard.

My brain feels like it's doing donuts in my skull. How can I ignore this? As we stand in the middle of the kitchen staring at each other, Joey coasts in carrying an empty glass. He steps past us to the refrigerator and pulls a tray of ice from the freezer. "Why is there blood all over the floor?"

AT DINNER, ALL I can think of is that word scribbled on my notepad.

Look.

It has to be a ghost. I mean, Dad and Joey don't even know about the dream, and even if they did, neither of them are the type to play pranks. So if it wasn't me and it wasn't Kerry . . .

We finish eating around seven, and Dad goes off to

watch his baseball pregame show. Since I always make Joey help with the dishes, he looks a little suspicious when I give him the night off. It isn't until Kerry explains that we're actually doing him a favor that he agrees, and we have the kitchen to ourselves. That one-word message has changed everything, and Joey can't know about it. He's such a blabbermouth.

"So, now that you've had time to think," Kerry says as she dries the dinner plate I just washed, "any opinions on who might have left that key? Your mum, maybe?"

"Maybe. But it could just as well by my grandma, or even Grandpa Joe."

"Hopefully, we'll find out when we go up there tonight." She raises an empty glass as if making a toast. "Here's to going to the third floor and recording the best evidence ever."

"But what if my dad catches us? And what if the floor really *is* dangerous?"

"Take a breath, Theresa." Just like she did in the basement, Kerry puts her arm around my shoulder and whispers in my ear, "We'll take every precaution, I promise. Your dad won't even know we've been up there. Besides, how big a secret can he be keeping? It's not as if there's some mad uncle chained to the wall up there. Who'd have been feeding him all these years?"

"I still don't feel good about this, Kerry." I wave off the idea with a soapy hand and go back to washing the dishes.

"Come on. This is a huge house, and we'll be two floors up. Like you said, he'll never bother us during a baseball game. Don't you want to know what that dream was about?"

"Obviously, I do, but we just can't. Something will happen. The Giants will hit a grand slam and he'll come running up to tell everybody."

"Blast." She strides over to the table and drops into a chair, elbows on the table, chin on her hands. "There has to be some way to do this without getting caught." The kitchen is so quiet I can hear the baseball commentator on Dad's TV from way across the house. I go back to scrubbing out the enchilada pan.

After a bit, Kerry stands up and pushes her chair back under the table. "I have a plan."

At the sight of her grinning face, a combination of dread and excitement flows through me, and I swallow. "Wha-what is it?"

CHAPTER 22

EVEN THOUGH IT'S a weekend and we're allowed to stay up late, Kerry and I say good night to Dad at ten thirty. But sleep isn't in our plans. We're heading up to get ready for what we hope will be our most exciting ghost-chasing adventure yet. If things go our way, we'll end up with a video worthy of the *Ghosters* two-hundred-thousand-dollar prize.

We reach the door to my room, and I leave Kerry and run down the hall to the bathroom. She's sitting on my bed when I get back, and frowns at the sight of the yellow bath towel I'm holding.

"What's that for?" she asks.

"Watch this." I shut the door and stuff the towel into the gap beneath.

"Don't tell me . . . you're a smoker."

"What? No! It's not to keep cigarette smoke in. I just don't want my dad to notice the light coming from under the door. We're supposed to be sleeping, you know."

Her eyes narrow. "Brilliant. You're quite the sneak, aren't you? Now, all we have to do is wait until he goes to bed. After that we'll slip up to the third floor like two little mice."

I lean over her, hands on hips. "And we're waiting until we're one hundred percent sure he's asleep, too. No guessing." *The last thing I need is him catching us up there.*

"Fine, fine." She pushes me away and heaves her bulging backpack up onto the bed. "Are you still sure you don't want Joey to come along? He really is a talented cameraman."

"Are you kidding? Rules are rules with him. He'd tell Dad for sure."

"I suppose so. You know him better than I do." She

reaches into her pack and places the EMF meter, the EVP recorder, and a small silver flashlight side by side on the bed.

I set my own flashlight beside hers. "I put fresh batteries in it."

"Good. These all have freshly charged batteries too."

"Yeah, but that won't matter if the ghost decides to drain them. Why can't it just take whatever energy it needs from the air? Isn't that why rooms turn cold when they're around? The ghost using up all the heat?"

"That's what I've been told. Perhaps draining batteries takes less effort. Anyway, I may have a solution for that." She unzips the small front pocket of her backpack and reaches in. This time she pulls out two clear plastic sandwich bags, which she holds up proudly. "We're going to bribe the ghosts."

What the heck? "With empty bags?"

"Of course not."

"Well, what are we going to fill them with, cookies?"

"No, with treats they'll appreciate even more."

She opens a different pocket of her backpack. I'm even more confused as she pulls out two big handfuls of batteries ranging from AAA to D size.

"There," she says after separating the batteries into two equal piles. "Some for you and some for me."

"I still don't get it."

"It's simple," she says, handing me one of the bags. "You zip your batteries into this, then tuck the top of the bag into your waistband."

"Oh, I see. The part with the batteries hangs out so the ghost can see them. It drains the energy it needs from those instead of from the batteries in our equipment." I give her a high-five. "Smart thinking."

"Thanks, and now . . ." Again, she reaches into her pack.

I feel like I'm watching a magic act. What's she going to pull out now?

"Surprise!" She raises her chin proudly. "It's a full-spectrum HD video camera. My uncle gave it to me. And not on loan, either. *To keep.* It's an early Christmas *and* birthday present."

"That means you won't have to use a flashlight anymore. You can see in the dark with that thing, right?"

She sets the camera down on the bed. "Yeah, but this isn't all I got." With a grin that nearly splits her face, she dips both hands into the backpack. "When I told Uncle Scott what we've been doing he decided to help, so he decided to loan me this." She pulls out a plastic case the size of a kid's lunch box and opens it. "This little fellow costs four thousand dollars."

To me, the thing looks like any other camera, but Kerry squeezes it to her chest like she's just won an Oscar. "It's a thermal infrared video camera. It shows the heat signature of things, and since ghosts are made of energy, they'll show up on this. You know, like rainbow colors. Billy Joe used one the other day on *Ghosters.*"

This is awesome. Now we'll both be able to see in the dark. I lay my hand on the first camera, the full-spectrum. "So, I get to use this one tonight?"

"Exactly."

"But I'm still taking my flashlight for backup. Oh, and don't forget your inhaler."

"Oh, yeah." She pulls one out of the backpack and sets in on the bed. "Are you one hundred percent sure you want to go through with this? I mean, I obviously am, but you have a lot more to lose than me."

I look down at the bed, where our collection of ghost-chasing tools range from plastic sandwich bags to an infrared camera worth thousands of dollars. "Yeah, I'm sure. It'll be fine. All we have to do is to wait for dad to go to bed."

CHAPTER 23

KERRY AND I find something quiet to do while we wait for Dad to come upstairs. Since she doesn't have to worry about draining the battery on her phone anymore Kerry lies on my bed playing *Fruit Frenzy*. I kick back in the big chaise longue with a paperback, an old afghan draped across my feet. But I can't focus on my reading. Everything that's happened and everything I hope will happen is circling through my head.

Once Dad sees our recordings, he'll have to believe. And if he admits ghost exist, then why not heaven? A chance to be with Mom someday could be just what he needs to snap out of his depression. After that, who knows? Maybe he'll start writing again.

Even with the possibility of all those good things, the idea of seeing another ghost makes me tremble. I tug the afghan up over me. Maybe it'll be less scary this time since I actually expect to see one. I stare at the book, stuck on the same page until the grandfather clock chimes the hour fifteen minutes later. Soon after, the stairs creak.

Dad's coming.

The way Kerry and I stare at the door, you'd think we have x-ray vision. After a few seconds, we hear a door shut, then water running and some bathroom sounds. Thankfully, the walls muffle most of them. After what seems like a lifetime, the door opens again. What if he can still see light even with the towel stuffed under my door? I hold my breath. Stupid. We should have turned the darned lamp off and sat in the dark. I imagine Dad glancing at my door, noticing a tiny sliver of light. He bursts in and freaks out over all the ghost stuff piled on the bed.

Of course, none of that happens. Like every other night, Dad heads straight to his room, which shares a wall with mine. I breathe easier when the door clicks shut behind him. Soon after, his mattress groans as he settles himself onto it. As far as he knows, we're snoozing away like two little lambs with Kerry on the trundle bed we've pulled out from beneath mine.

By eleven ten, Kerry's asleep. By eleven twenty, Dad's snoring away. After a while I set aside my book and glasses and poke Kerry.

"He's sleeping now," I say, voice lowered.

"How do you . . . ?" At the sound of Dad's snoring, her head swivels toward it. "What's he doing in there? Cutting firewood with a chain saw?"

I shrug. What I can't believe is how she could nod off knowing what we're about to do.

Once Kerry blinks herself awake, she turns on the EVP recorder, clips it onto her waistband, then carefully hangs the four-thousand-dollar video camera around her neck by the strap.

I do the same with the full-spectrum HD camera and, since Joey won't be with us, stuff the EMF meter into my back pocket. We tuck the top of a battery-filled sandwich bag into our waistbands, leaving the contents to hang visible on the outside. We clip the flashlights to our belts. Kerry pockets her inhaler, and we're ready to go. What am I forgetting?

After a little digging around in my closet, I come out holding my old softball bat. Kerry looks at me like I'm nuts, so I motion for her to bend down. "This isn't for the ghosts," I whisper into her ear. "It's for the cobwebs. They're all over the stairs."

She mimes a long *Ooooooooh* and gives me a thumbs-up. Then she holds up my glasses, another thing I forgot.

Since I'll need those when I use the full spectrum camera, I perch them on my head for later.

Okay, this is it. I toss aside the towel I stuffed under the door, lay my hand on the doorknob, and in my softest voice say, "Let's go win two hundred thousand dollars."

Kerry taps me on the shoulder.

I look up at her, eyebrows raised. What now?

She's pointing at my desk.

The key to the third floor is sitting in the middle of it. Come on, Theresa. Get it together. I shoulder my way past Kerry and grab the key, then hold it above my head like a tiny little sword. "*Now*, let's go win two—"

With a shush and a push, my speech is cut short.

She's right. The less noise we make, the better. I turn off my bedroom light and open the door.

The sound of Dad's snoring leaks out into the hallway, but it's Joey's softer higher pitched rumble that widens Kerry's eyes.

Whatever. For all I know, I do it too.

We troop toward the door to the third floor, shoes *swishing* along the carpet runner. The rest of the house is dark, but here, tall and short shadows bob in the glow of the night light Dad set out for me.

We get to the end of the hallway, and I lean the softball bat against the wall. Then, it hits me. For the first time in my life I'm completely ignoring Dad's orders. Not that I'm a perfect angel. I've done stuff. But mostly my sins are minor, like taking my brother's Halloween candy and not brushing my teeth. Never anything big . . . like this.

If we're selected as finalists, Dad's obviously going to find out. He'll be mad, but he'll want that money. Heck, he needs that money. Anyway, it's for his own good, and that secret he's keeping can't be that big of a deal.

Satisfied I'm doing the right thing, I slide the key into the lock. It turns easily. I swing the door open and it makes an eye-bulging creak.

We freeze.

The snoring stops. Kerry glares first at me, then at the now silent hallway.

I signal for her to wait then look that way too. Come on, guys. It takes more than a little door creaking to get you two out of bed.

After a few seconds, Joey starts up again, then Dad.

"Get the WD-40," Kerry whispers. "That door's going to squeak again when we close it."

I nod. The servants' stairs are right there, so I flick on my flashlight and slip down them. Having stored the spray can in the pantry, I'm back in less than a minute. After a few squirts on the hinges, we step inside.

Even though the door is open all the way, it's as dark as a movie theater in there. The smell reminds me of the house on the day we moved in, dusty and abandoned.

Kerry turns on her thermal infrared camera. She points it at the staircase, and I lean in for a look. The three-inch screen is filled with bright shades of purple, blue, turquoise, and green. She motions me toward the stairs, and I step in front of her.

"You look awesome," she whispers. "Your body heat makes you show up red, orange, and yellow."

Anxious to start using the full-spectrum camera, I pull out the EMF meter.

Nothing.

I give Kerry the thumbs-down signal we agreed would mean no ghost action. Then I turn it around to check the temperature.

Sixty-seven degrees. Cool, but nothing weird.

Kerry passes me the softball bat and waves me up the stairs. As planned, she keeps a lookout for ghosts with the infrared while I knock down the webs.

With one hand waving the bat and the other gripping the banister, using the camera will have to wait as I inch up the dark staircase, hopefully, tearing down cobwebs. After a dozen steps, I check the EMF meter again. Even though I can barely see Kerry, I give her another thumbs-down. Hopefully, she sees it on her camera screen.

I'm creeped out by so much darkness, and my hands are

sweaty, especially the one gripping the banister. Lucky for me, this one is tons sturdier than the one in the basement. At the top of the stairs I wave the bat around some more, then scurry back down the stairs.

"Slow down," Kerry whispers. "It's not safe to run in the dark like that."

"Who's running in the dark?" Like a little sprite, Joey pops out from behind Kerry.

Freaked by Joey's surprise appearance, the bat slips from my hand and bounces off the floor with a clatter.

Kerry gasps and spins around. "Joey, what are you doing here?"

"I'm standing," he answers in his normal speaking voice.

I want to jump on him, cover his mouth with my hand. Knowing that will only make things worse, I press one finger to my own lips. "Shhh!" Even in the dim light, I can see that he's looking right at me. "Joey, we—"

"You promised you wouldn't come in here again." At least he lowered his voice.

"Yeah, but the—"

"I'm telling Dad." He turns around.

Before he takes two steps, Kerry grabs his tee-shirt and yanks him back inside with us. I click on my flashlight and push the door most of the way shut.

He glares down at the floor. "I don't like when people touch me."

"Please, Joey, keep it down," Kerry begs, palms pressed together. "I'm truly sorry, but give us a chance to explain."

"Explain what?" Even though his voice is softer, it's obvious he's angry. To my surprise, he looks right at me. "Why are you in here? Dad specifically said—"

"Jojo . . ." Kerry reaches for him but stops. "Things aren't always black and white."

All the eye contact must be too much for him, because his gaze drops to the circle of light my flashlight is throwing on the floor. "Why is Kerry talking about old-timey TV shows?"

I push between them. "No, Joey, not TV shows. Kerry means that sometimes things aren't a hundred percent right or a hundred percent wrong. Remember that key we found in the basement?"

"Yes, you used it to get in here."

"That's right, but you know where we found it?"

"In the basement. I was with you, remember?"

Not wanting to lose my cool, I stop and take a breath. "I meant *after* that. Kerry found it lying in the middle of my desk."

"So?"

"It was sitting on a piece of paper that said *LOOK*." I lay my hand on his shoulder. "I didn't put the key there, Jojo. And I didn't write that word either. A ghost did."

For a while he studies the floor. Then he shrugs off my hand and points up the stairs. "So the ghost wants you to see what's up there?"

"That's what we think."

"But Dad doesn't want us to do that. We could get hurt. He was very precise."

Kerry blinks hard, obviously frustrated by this pause in the action. "And we know that, but we aren't planning on stomping all over the place." Even though she's anxious to get going, she still manages to make the words come out soft, slow. "We'll just creep up to the top of the stairs and have a look. Theresa's already gone up and back once, and the stairs were perfectly safe. Isn't that right, Theresa?"

I nod. "Yeah, Jojo. Not even squeaky." I pull the EMF meter from my pocket and offer it to him. "Here. We'll probably be finished in five minutes."

He stares at the EMF meter as if taking it is equal to signing a contract with the devil. "I don't think so . . ."

"Please, Joey. If you tell Dad, I'll get in trouble. Then, there'll be no more ghost chasing. Maybe even no more Kerry. Ever. Do you want that?" Maybe I'm exaggerating, but what choice do I have?

After more than a few seconds, he accepts the EMF meter, and Kerry starts breathing again.

I pick up the softball bat. "Thanks, Joey, and don't worry. Everything's going to be fine."

Since I don't trust the lock, I lay the bat on the floor between the door and the frame, allowing a thin crack of light to leak through. The full-spectrum camera hangs against my chest, and I turn it on.

"Thanks for letting me use this," I tell Kerry. "Everything's super clear, so who cares if the picture's in black and white."

"That's yours, Kerry?" Joey leans in to see. "It's like watching an episode of *I Love Lucy.*"

"I got it from my uncle." She holds up the thermal infrared camera. "He loaned me this camera too. Check it out."

Joey squints at the screen, and the hint of a smile touches his lips. "I like that." He eyeballs the bags of batteries hanging from our waistbands, but doesn't ask.

Kerry huddles us all together. "All right," she whispers. "I'll go first. Joey, you can walk alongside Theresa and share her camera." She looks from Joey to me. "That all right?"

We both nod. I click off the flashlight. My camera screen shows wood paneled walls, just like the ones in the main hallway, along with the same worn-out carpet runner.

Kerry stops halfway up. "Anything on the EMF, Joey?"

"Nothing."

"Hang on. I want to try something." I pull the bag of batteries from my belt and hold it up. "Hey, ghost?" I say in a hard whisper. "See these batteries? We'd really appreciate if when you need some extra energy, you take it from these, and not from the ones in our equipment."

Kerry holds hers up to, and Joey watches as we wave the bags over our heads.

"Nothing's happening," he whispers.

"We don't know that," Kerry says. "A ghost could have drained every single one of them. How would we know?"

She tucks the bag back in her waistband. "Never mind. Let's keep going."

We make our way to the top without any more stops. Once there, my camera reveals a square landing much larger than the one at the base of the stairs, surrounded by four closed doors. In the middle of the dusty hardwood floor is a square floral rug, and on top of that, a round table with thick legs ending in lion's paws. I lower the camera. On the far wall is a floor-to-ceiling stained glass window, all dull reds and oranges in the moonlight.

Other than some dust and a chandelier covered with cobwebs, the place seems like any other part of the house.

"So, where's all the mess?" Kerry asks, scanning the area with her video camera. "The way your dad told it, we should be crashing through the floor with every step we take."

I shake my head. I'm as confused as you are.

Joey holds up the EMF meter to get our attention. "One of the lights is lit now."

"Good," Kerry says. "But remember, that could just be bad wiring." She bounces on her toes. The floor seems solid, not even a creak. After taking a few steps, she does it again.

"Hey," I reach out. "You promised you wouldn't . . ."

Kerry ignores me and strides toward the stained glass window. I can barely feel the vibration. I don't get it. There's nothing wrong with this floor . . . is there?

"Come on, Kerry. My dad said—"

"Yes, I remember." She turns in slow circles, filming. "It looks like your dad was misinformed. This floor is actually quite sturdy."

Before I can stop him, Joey heads over to Kerry and does some bouncing of his own.

"It's true," he says. "There's nothing wrong with this floor."

Was Dad lying to us all the time? Why in the world would he do that? Out of the blue, my skin starts to tingle like a gang of invisible ants are crawling up my arms.

"Either of you guys feel weird?" I ask.

"Yeah," Joey says. "It's probably because of the four lights on the EMF meter."

I turn slowly, scanning the room with my camera. "I don't see anything."

"It's over here," Kerry says in a raspy voice that makes me hold my breath. "Turn around, Theresa . . . slowly."

CHAPTER 24

EYES STILL ON my camera screen, I do what Kerry asks and gasp. Across the wide third floor landing, it looks like steam is seeping out of the wall.

"Do you see it?" she whispers.

"I . . . I see it." Since I'd rather not stand alone, I move closer to Joey, who's studying the screen of Kerry's infrared camera like it's one of his bug videos. Kerry holds it so I can see too. A circle of red and white heat the size of a baseball hovers a foot or so off the floor.

Even though the room is almost black, the glow from the camera screens gives off just enough light for us to see each other's faces. Joey leans in to look at my black-and-white screen.

"On Theresa's it looks like a ball of dust," he says matter-of-factly.

Oh my god, this is really happening. "It's getting bigger." I say it in a whisper even though I feel like screaming. A tiny moan still leaks out. Keep it together, Theresa.

With Joey pressed between us, Kerry and I keep recording. Once the vapor finishes oozing from the wall, it changes shape: first a head, then a torso, and two arms. But no detail, like something a kid might shape from a ball of clay. A swirling mist takes the place of legs.

Joey takes a step closer, hands on his hips. "Not very big, is it?"

He's right. The thing is barely as tall as the lion's paw table. Maybe it's the same little ghost I saw in Grandma Carmen's wardrobe.

I glance up from the screen to look at it with my own eyes. Nothing. Just a dark empty room.

What the . . . ? Whoa! Without Kerry's camera I wouldn't even know if—holy crabs! How many times has that thing stood beside me and I didn't even know it? I shiver at the idea.

Kerry's staring bug-eyed, her brand-new inhaler glued to her lips. As usual, Joey's as calm as a sleeping puppy.

"Why are you scared?" he asks me. "It's so little, and Kerry said they can't hurt us."

The ghost raises an arm, signaling for us to come closer. None of us moves, and it glides silently toward us.

"Oh, cool . . ." Joey says.

Kerry steps aside.

But the little ghost doesn't seem to care about either one of them. It's coming toward me. My trembling hands clutch the camera in a death grip. With my heart ready to explode, I shuffle back toward the stairs, pulling my brother with me.

"Let me go," Joey insists as he peels my fingers from his arm. "It wants you, not me."

Not exactly the protective brother I was hoping for. Luckily, the ghost doesn't come any closer. It stares at me, and even though its eyes are no more than dark craters I get the feeling it's disappointed.

"Wha-what do we do now?" I ask Kerry, unable to tear my eyes from the tiny black-and-white screen in front of me.

"Just keep filming . . . please."

So, even though my stomach feels like I swallowed a bucket of snakes, that's what I do. And that's fine if the ghost would just stay put, but no. My breath catches as it starts to move. To my relief, this time it heads toward one of the four doors that surround us.

"Where's it going?" Joey asks.

I take deep breaths, hoping to slow my heart down. The spirit stops at the door and turns. Again it looks right at me, and again, the ants are marching up my arms, but this time in rows of tens and twenties.

"I think it wants Theresa to follow it," Kerry says.

"Me? H-how do you know?"

The little ghost raises a blurry arm, signaling.

"That," says Joey.

Holy crabs! It does want me to follow it. I lick my lips. "Kerry . . . ?"

When it sees I'm staying put, the ghost shoulders seem to slump, and it turns toward the door. I watch, open mouthed, as the thing appears to soak into the closed door and disappear.

"The EMF meter still has three lights lit," Joey says. "I think it's still on the other side . . . waiting for you."

"You should open that door," Kerry whispers.

Even though I'd rather eat a bowl of worms, she's right. That ghost wants me to see what's back there. But what could it be? And why me? I haven't been in this house since I was a baby. And never up here.

With a sigh, I creep across the space between me and the door. It makes sense that we open it. But I'm in no hurry.

Kerry grips her inhaler, so excited she's practically vibrating. "Do you want me to?"

"No, I can do it." Slowly, I step closer. Barely breathing, I lay my hand on the doorknob. Kerry gives me a "be careful" nod. That's when I get the feeling someone is right behind us. Another ghost? Before I can turn around, the chandelier blazes on. Blinded, I shriek. Kerry too.

"What the heck are you kids doing up here?"

Hearing my dad's voice surprises me, and I scream again as he jerks me away from the door. Two big hands grab my thrashing arms and pin them to my sides.

"Calm down!" Dad shouts.

Kerry and Joey squint and blink, their mouths hanging open. With his dark hair sticking out in all directions and dressed only in a tee-shirt and gym shorts, Dad looks almost as scared as they do.

"What happened?" he asks me, all buggy-eyed.

I throw my arms around him. "We saw a ghost."

"A ghost, huh?" He moves away from the door. Still hugging, I stumble along with him. "Where?"

Joey points at the empty floor, then at the door.

Dad raises my chin with his finger. "Have you been in there?"

I shake my head, and his expression changes from scared to relieved, and he returns my hug, his big arms pressing my head to his chest.

What's with him?

He turns to Joey. "So, nobody went in there?"

"Theresa was going to," Joey answers, "but—"

"But I scared you," Dad finishes, looking a little guilty.

"Not me." Joey points. "Those two were the scared ones."

The wrinkles on Dad's forehead smooth as he watches Joey step to the wall and rub his hand across the fuzzy red wallpaper. Then he notices all the gadgets we're toting.

"What's all this stuff? Kerry, is it yours?"

"Mostly. All except for this one." She holds up the thermal camera. "It's my uncle's."

Dad turns back to me and frowns. "How did you guys get in here?"

He drills me with his eyes, and my gaze drops. "I found the key in Grandpa's workshop the other day."

"And you kept it a secret. Didn't I tell you not to come up here? I told you it was dangerous."

"But it's not," Kerry blurts.

With the look Dad gives her, she probably wishes she could suck the words back into her mouth.

"Yeah, well . . . I've never actually been up here, so . . ." Dad turns away from us, and Kerry's gaze ping pongs between me and him.

Dad turns to me, with one hand out, palm up. "Give me the key."

I dig it out of my pocket, and he takes it.

"Even though this place doesn't look dangerous, it is," he says, pointing at the door we'd watched the little ghost pass through just minutes ago. "And that room especially. I uh . . . remember your grandfather warning me about it."

"But the ghost," Kerry sputters. "It wanted us to go in there."

"What?" Dad scowls at Kerry. "That's impossible."

Joey and I nod.

"It was really little," Joey said. He holds his hand out, palm down. "Some little kid must have died here back before Grandpa and Grandma Ramos bought the house."

Dad's jaw drops. "Y-you saw . . . no, you couldn't have."

"I think Mom might be involved," I blurt out. "I had this dream the other night, and she—"

"Okay," Dad says, chest heaving. "Stop it right there."

He squeezes his eye shut, and the three of us watch as he draws in several deep breaths, calming himself. He finally opens his eyes, and a stiff smile creeps across his lips.

"You kids really need to get your imaginations under control. Come on, we're leaving." He starts herding us all back down the stairs.

"But I recorded it." I turn back, hold up my camera. I even try to stop, but he's not having it. Strong hands turn me around. They press on my back as we head back downstairs.

"You didn't see any ghosts," Dad tells us. "You kids were all pumped up with adrenaline. You just *imagined* you saw one." He chuckles, but there's no humor in his voice. "Go to bed, girls, and leave Joey out of it from now on."

Once we're all out in the main hallway, I spin around, trying to hand him the camera. "Sorry, Dad, but you're wrong. We really did see a ghost. I recorded it on this camera, and Kerry got it on hers too. Don't you want to see?"

Dad swings the door to the third floor shut and locks it. "Right now I want you all to go to bed. We'll deal with this in the morning. And no more noise, okay? I mean it."

Eventually, Kerry and I do go to bed, but not until after we see what we've recorded.

CHAPTER 25

THE NEXT MORNING, Joey, Kerry, and I are sitting around the kitchen table eating pancakes as Dad surprises us by marching in the back door. We didn't even know he had gone out. Without saying a word, he drops a small brown paper bag on the counter and heads down to the basement.

"What's Dad doing?" Joey asks.

"I don't know." I wave him toward the stairs. "Go look."

Since Dad has taken care of all the problems in the basement, it's safe now, and Joey takes the steps two at a time. While he's gone, I take a peek in the bag.

"It's a combination lock and one of those things you screw onto the wall to hook them through."

"You mean a hasp?" Kerry asks.

"I guess." I hold up the hinged hunk of metal.

After a couple of minutes, Joey trots back up the stairs. "Dad's in Grandpa's workshop looking for a drill. He says he's going to lock up the third floor so nobody can ever get in there again."

I pick up my empty plate. "That's okay. Last night we got two good recordings. If those don't win the *Ghosters* contest, nothing will."

ONCE WE'VE TAKEN care of the breakfast dishes, Kerry and I head up to my room. Dad's pretty good with tools, so the new lock is already in place when we get there.

"Crikey," Kerry says as we peer down the hall at the shiny silver-and-black lock. "Your dad must really be peeved."

"You got that right," I mutter.

I pad across my bedroom, grab my laptop, and plop

down in the big chaise longue in the corner. After a few clicks, the *Ghosters* website fills my screen. The contest info takes up half of the main page.

"Are you sure you still want to do this?" Kerry asks. "Your dad never gave you permission to enter the contest."

How can I explain that I'm doing this for Dad's own good, as well as my own? I smile up at her. "He never said I couldn't."

"You're starting to sound like me." Kerry pulls the infrared camera out of her backpack and pops out the memory chip.

"I bet they've gotten a thousand submissions," I say, scrolling down.

"Doesn't matter. Ours have to be the best." She hovers alongside me as one at a time, our little treasures are successfully uploaded to the *Ghosters* website.

The word *NEXT* appears in a little box on the screen.

I click on it, and there's all our info, including the names of both our files. Satisfied I've inputted everything correctly, I smile up at Kerry and move the mouse over the word *SUBMIT*.

What the heck? In a flash, my grin morphs into a big fat scowl. Right above the big yellow *SUBMIT* button there's a little square and these words beside it: By clicking this box you acknowledge that you are over eighteen years of age.

"Blast," Kerry says. "Looks like we're out."

"No we aren't." I move the cursor over the yellow button.

"We're not eighteen, Theresa."

"So?" Since Kerry's looming over me like a six-foot-two vulture, I turn things around by hopping up on the chaise longue and look down on her for a change. "*They* don't know we're not eighteen. I mean, what's the worst that can happen? They don't pick us as finalists?"

"No, the worst thing would be that they *do* pick us as finalists. My parents don't mind my ghost chasing, but yours . . ." She throws up her arms. "It's bad enough that we're entering the contest without your dad's permission, but what do you think he'll do if those *Ghosters* vans pull up in your driveway and Tyson O'Seanesey gets out looking for a grown-up Theresa and Kerry?"

I shrug. "You look pretty grown up to me."

She takes a step back, giggling at the sight of me. "Come down here. I've got an idea how we can even this height thing out."

We lie on the bed, our heads side by side. Hands clasped over our chests, we stare up at the glow-in-the-dark stars I glued to the ceiling.

I speak first. "The way I see it, even if the *Ghosters* do show up, what's my dad going to do? Chase them away with a shotgun? He might yell at me, but he never goes off on strangers. Anyway, he needs money, and that's an awful lot of cash to slam a door on."

"But what about the Ghosters? They'll—"

"They'll be mad when they find out we lied, but I doubt if they'll come all this way just to turn around and go home. We just have to pray that Tyson O'Seanesey can talk Dad into letting them in."

"But what if your dad *doesn't* allow the Ghosters inside?"

A few feet away on my pillow, Frankie the bear watches and listens. I drag him over and tuck him under my arm. "That's a risk I'm willing to take. I'm tired of seeing him this way, Kerry. He can't write . . . He—he can't support us. And he's always grumpy. Winning this contest could change all of that." I'm also hoping the win will make Dad like me more, but that's something I'm not ready to share yet.

"Well, you know what I want."

"Then I'm doing it." I get up and click the *SUBMIT* button. Even though I've just added another lie to my growing list, it feels right.

CHAPTER 26

TO MY SURPRISE, two weeks pass and we still haven't heard from the *Ghosters* people. Kerry stays positive. She thinks we haven't heard from them yet because they've received more submissions than they expected. I'm not so sure. As Dad always says, there's always somebody out there who can beat you.

With no ghost activity since the night Dad caught us up on the third floor, and no news from the contest, I try to put the whole thing out of my mind. But Kerry's still a ghost nut, and every Wednesday afternoon we sprawl out on the living room sofa to watch *Ghosters*, followed by *Paranormal Pets*.

"Why do we even watch this stupid pet show?" I ask her.

"I think it's fun."

"It's about the ghosts of dead dogs and cats coming back to haunt their masters. They don't even have images, just noises and smells."

"You forget last week's episode. Remember when that old woman had her hand licked? That would totally freak me out."

I giggle. "True, but human ghosts are better."

"Why do you say that?"

"They don't smell like dog poop."

That one earns me a pillow to the face. My return throw misses Kerry completely, grazing the lamp on the end table behind her. Terrified, I watch it wobble. But before Grandma's lamp crashes onto the floor, Kerry grabs it just as a loud buzz makes the phone rattle halfway across the coffee table. I spring up as if electrocuted. "What if it's *Ghosters* calling?"

Kerry steadies the lamp and gives me a shove. "So, answer it and find out, silly."

I push the button and hold the receiver to my ear, face scrunching from the stress.

"Hello?" The word comes out a squeak.

"Hello, my name is Debbie Langston. I'm secretary to Mr. Tyson O'Seanesey, executive producer of *Ghosters*. May I please speak to either Theresa Martinez or Kerry Sullivan?"

My mouth opens in a silent scream, and I bunny hop across the room.

"Hello? Are you still there?" Debbie Langston asks.

Kerry bops me on the back of the head. "Say something, you twit."

The smack yanks me back to reality. "Th-this is Theresa Martinez."

"Theresa, your recordings have been selected as one of the three finalists in the *Ghosters* Halloween Contest, and Mr. O'Seanesey would like to schedule a date for the team to explore the location of your manifestation. Would that be all right?"

"Sure," I tell her, then grin at Kerry. "I'd love for the *Ghosters* team to explore my house."

"Great. Your online submission form says the location of the manifestation is the same as your mailing address. Is that correct?"

Like an idiot, I nod.

"Speak," Kerry pleads.

I nod harder. "Yes, yes, that's right. We recorded it upstairs."

"That's wonderful. Mr. O'Seanesey and the team are very excited to experience your apparition first hand." She pauses. "Um . . . Theresa, your submission also states that you're over eighteen years of age. Is that correct?"

Lying on the Internet was so much easier. As Kerry would say, blast.

"Theresa . . . ? Are you still there?"

"Yes, hold on." I put my hand over the phone. Kerry's looking at me like I'm the biggest dork she's ever seen. I glare at her. "She wants to know if I'm really over eighteen," I whisper.

"Tell her yes."

I clear my throat then speak in the most grown-up voice I can manage. "I'm sorry . . . the uh . . . dog had a little accident. You were saying?"

"I asked if you were over eighteen." Debbie Langston chuckles. "You, uh, sound a little young, if you don't mind me saying."

"Oooooh, don't you worry . . . I'm legal." I cringe at just how phony I sound, but plow ahead anyway. "You'd be amazed at how often I get that. No, I'm far from being eighteen."

Even though my heart is pounding a mile a minute, Debbie must be convinced, because she gives me a good laugh for that. Within a few minutes we've arranged for the *Ghosters* to show up at ten p.m. Saturday night. All the while, Kerry is looking at me with a mixture of half-respect and half-shock.

"That was amazing," she says, once Debbie and I say our goodbyes.

I imagine a cartoon with a big snowball tumbling down mountain. The ball takes out everything in its path: squirrels . . . rabbits—even trees. Everything sticks, and the ball grows and grows.

"What's the matter?" Kerry asks. "I should think you'd be happy."

"I'm not sure. I mean, yeah, I'm glad we were selected, but the lying. It was fun while I was doing it, but now . . ." My shoulders sag. "I feel greasy, like I need a shower, but on the inside."

"Forget all that that. We've been selected. We're going to be on television." To my surprise, she takes my hands and jumps up and down. "And when we win, we'll be famous and rich, rich, rich."

"Woohoo!" I shout.

Kerry pulls me out into the middle of the room and we do a few spins and hops, shouting and laughing. Like all the other unpleasant things in my life, I try to sweep the little scam I played on Debbie Langston aside. This time I hide it under something good, the chance to hand my father a check for $100,000.

Dad's at the store, but Joey's upstairs, and the noise brings him out of his room. We hear him on the stairs, and we quit all the hopping and drop back onto the sofa like puppets that just had their strings cut. I click the TV back on and switch to Animal Planet.

"What were you two doing?" Joey asks, already eyeballing the TV screen.

Lucky for me, there's some kind of huge beetle rolling what looks like a baseball-sized ball of mud down a dirt road. I learned about them in sixth grade. It's an Egyptian dung beetle.

Joey parks himself on the edge of Dad's recliner, elbows on knees, chin balanced on his fists.

The last thing Kerry and I want is for Joey to know the Ghosters will be here in two days. He'd never agree to keep the secret, and even if he did, I know it would slip out. Unlike me, the kid's too darned honest. I look at Kerry.

"Hey, Joey," she says, giving me a wink. "You know a lot about insects and such. What type of creature is that?"

"A dung beetle," he answers, eyes never leaving the screen.

"And what's that thing it's rolling?"

"A ball of poop."

Even though we never told Joey why we were bouncing on the sofa, Kerry's questions seem to have wiped it from his mind. Do sins still count if they're done for a good reason? I squeeze my eyes shut and pray that they don't. Saturday night can't come soon enough.

CHAPTER 27

ON THE BIG night, I get permission for Kerry to sleep over again. Dad agrees, but only after I've promised him not to do anymore ghost chasing. It's not exactly a lie, since we have a good idea where the ghost will be, but close enough that the greasy feeling comes back. Since I'm way too excited to cook, I mention to Joey that I'm planning on making his most hated dish, chow mein. As I expect, he talks Dad into ordering pizza.

Dad always eats a bunch of pizza, and even though Joey has to take it completely apart before eating, he has no trouble finishing three slices. Kerry's stomach must be fluttery, because she barely finishes one. And me? I can't even gag down a glass of soda, never mind the pizza. Lucky for me, nobody notices, and after a sorry attempt at dinner, we leave Dad in the living room and Kerry and I accept Joey's invitation to play his favorite video game, *Real-Pro Wrestling*, upstairs in his room. We're both too wound up to focus, and after an hour of being body-slammed by Joey, we head downstairs, leaving him to play solo.

Even though the Ghosters aren't due till ten, at eight p.m. the two of us are already staring out the front window. Along with the Ghosters, we're also waiting for the first big rainstorm of the season. Dad sits in his usual spot on the recliner behind us, watching his baseball.

"Worried about the storm?" he calls out during a commercial.

"Nah. Just interested." I peer up at the steel-gray sky, then turn and make myself smile. "Why?"

"You girls look nervous. All night you guys have been acting like long-tailed cats in a roomful of rocking chairs."

"The clouds are really getting thick," I say. "Bet it starts coming down any minute."

Not wanting to look any more suspicious than we already do, I drag Kerry away from the window. Joey's sitting in the middle of the sofa eating ice cream, so we plop down on either side of him. Who cares if it's just baseball on the TV? No matter what show is on, we're in no shape to follow it.

"I'm curious," Joey says, balancing the bowl on his lap. "Where would a cat find a roomful of rocking chairs?"

I roll my eyes, too nervous to explain Dad's weak joke.

After what seems like fifty years, my heart skips at the sound of wheels on gravel. Kerry and I have our noses pasted to the front window when the two big *Ghosters* vans pull to a stop, the first sprinkles of rain dotting their windshields. I recognize them from the show, but anyone with eyes can figure out what they are. Both vans are painted bright purple with the *Ghosters* logo across the side, a glowing green ghost under a giant magnifying glass. And as if that isn't enough, the word GHOSTERS and WE BELIEVE circle the spirit in huge letters that seem to glow supernaturally.

Three people get out of the first van, raising umbrellas. One, I recognize. It's Erin, the pink-haired Junior Ghoster. She's scowling, probably because the rain is starting and she's in charge of bringing all the computer stuff into the house.

Dad pushes in between Kerry and me as two slightly older guys climb out of the second van and begin giving instructions to the other three. "Why are all those people here?"

I lick my lips. "Th-they're the crew from *Ghosters*, Dad. See the one with all the tattoos? That's Billy Joe Francisco." Joey's still back on the sofa, so I call to him, "Jojo, d-don't you want to see the Ghosters?"

He loads his spoon with ice cream. "Are they going to come inside?"

"Well, yeah, I hope so, but—"

Dad's staring at me, eyebrows pushed together like two warring caterpillars. "Theresa Martinez, what have you done?" He frowns at the scene in the driveway, then back at me.

"Crikey!" Kerry shouts, ecstatic over the show outside. "Tyson O'Seanesey is looking at me."

Preferring not to maintain eye contact with my dad, I turn back to the window. Tyson, younger than Dad but about the same height, is squinting up at the house. His dark spiky hair reminds me of a cartoon character who's just seen a ghost. Dressed in his usual black jeans and tee-shirt, he waves and smiles as he pulls on a hoodie.

Kerry starts to run for the door, but stops. She looks back at me and my dad, hands clasped behind her.

This is what I've been dreading. It's time to explain things. I step away from the window, struggle to make eye contact with my father, who's glaring down on me, arms crossed.

"Dad . . . ?" Why did I think this would be easy? Again, I run my tongue over my lips and take a deep breath. "Remember the recordings Kerry and I made up on the third floor? The Ghosters are here because we entered those recordings in their video contest."

"What?" Dad looks at me like I've just told him I've joined the army. "You didn't record any ghosts."

Someone knocks at the door. Nobody moves to open it. In fact, it's so quiet I can hear Joey's spoon clinking against his bowl as he scrapes up another mouthful of ice cream.

Kerry shuffles toward us, hands tucked into the back pockets of her jeans. "But we did, Mr. Martinez, remember? You refused to look at our recordings."

Dad tromps toward the door. "Well, I don't care. I'm not having that bunch of ghost huggers roaming around my house." He throws open the door and there stands a smiling Tyson O'Seanesey, raindrops dotting his blue sweatshirt. He tucks a clipboard under his arm, dries his hand on his jeans, then sticks it out, ready to shake. "Hi there. Tyson O'Seanesey from *Ghosters*. I'm looking for Theresa Martinez and Kerry Sullivan."

Dad ignores the hand. "How can you just show up like this?" he growls. "Don't you need parental permission?"

Kerry and I edge closer, peeking around him.

Since Billy Joe Francisco has just reached the top of the steps, Tyson turns to him. "Hey, Billy, it sounds like Theresa and Kerry are this guy's kids."

Billy looks at Dad and grins. "Dude. You're their dad?" Even though it's sprinkling, all Billy's wearing is his classic "Billy Joe" outfit, a brilliant white sleeveless undershirt, and knee length cargo shorts, both speckled with raindrops. Except for Billy's face, tattoos cover every inch of him.

"Just Theresa's," Dad answers. "And I'm not some young looking old guy. The girls are twelve."

I grab Kerry's hand and squeeze it hard.

"Twelve?" Billy uses his hand to squeegee the mist dotting his shaved head. Down in the driveway, the three Junior Ghosters huddle beneath their umbrellas.

"Yeah, twelve," Dad says. "Sorry if you folks have traveled a long way to get here. It looks like we've *all* been tricked." He grabs the door and starts to close it.

"Wait. Let's talk. Maybe we can work this out." Tyson places his palm on the door, stopping it from closing.

"I doubt it," Dad says. "I am *not* having my kid on any fake ghost chasing programs."

"Mister Martinez," Tyson dips his chin and looks at Dad as if he's peering over the top of invisible glasses, "*Ghosters* is totally on the level, I assure you."

Since it doesn't look like they're going to work things out by themselves, I step out from behind my dad, pulling Kerry with me.

"Sorry for tricking you into coming here, Mr. O'Seanesey. We said we were eighteen because my dad doesn't believe in ghosts, and we knew he wouldn't have . . ."

Thunder rumbles in the distance. With the look Dad

gives me I leave the sentence half said and stare out at the pouring rain.

"You're right," he tells me. "I would never have let you enter that contest."

"Not even if you could win $100,000?" Billy asks through the shrinking gap.

Lightning flashes as Dad tugs the door back open. It's all Kerry and I can do not to scream.

"What are you talking about?" Dad asks. "How could some stupid kid video be worth that much money?"

"First prize is actually $200,000," Billy says. "But it's a shared submission. Haven't you seen the recordings? They're incredible."

"No, I, uh . . ." Dad clears his throat, coughs into his hand.

"They're the best pieces of paranormal evidence Tyson and I have ever seen." He looks at Kerry and me and winks.

Maybe this is going to work out after all. I cross my fingers. Heck, I'd cross my toes too if my shoes would let me.

"Please," Tyson says. "We really have driven a long way. Across five states, if you want to know. So if it's alright, may Billy and I *please* come in? We won't take up too much of your time."

"Oh, all right." With a sigh, Dad lets the door swing wide. "But just because the rain's starting to fall a lot harder now. Tell your crew they can come up on the porch."

"Thanks. Billy, tell the guys."

As Billy calls the crew up out of the rain, Tyson sticks his hand out to me. "Theresa?"

I nod and giggle as we shake. OMG, they're here. They're really here.

As if reading my mind, he grins. "You must be Kerry." Again, he offers his hand. Since she has him by at least five inches, Tyson has to look up at her, but the smile he gives her is just as bright as the one I got, and Kerry's knees bend like old shoe laces.

Once he's got us thoroughly melted, Tyson focuses on my dad. "You have an amazing house here, Mister Martinez."

"Thanks." Dad waves us all into the living room. "Have a seat."

I huddle next to Kerry on the love seat. With Joey still sitting in the middle of the sofa, Billy Joe and Tyson take the spots on either side of him.

"Hi, Tyson O'Seanesey." He holds his hand out to Joey, who looks at it as he continues to eat his ice cream.

"That's Joey," I explain, hugging a throw pillow to my chest. "He's . . . he's my brother."

Tyson nods and turns to Dad. "Mr. Martinez, please allow me and my crew to explore your home. If we experience anything like what we saw on the girls' recordings, they'll win our contest, hands down."

Dad sits on the edge of his recliner, hands clasped between his knees. "I'm sorry, but it all seems like a scam to me. I've been living here for weeks, and I haven't seen anything unusual. Those recordings must have been some sort of trick of the light, a reflection."

"You could be right," Tyson says. "But isn't it worth a few hours of your time to find out?"

Dad peers at me. The look makes me feel like a convicted murderer waiting for sentencing. I can't help but squirm. God, what's he thinking?

"Fine, you can look," he mutters as if the words taste bad.

It worked! I want to scream, bounce on the sofa. From the look on Kerry's face, she does too. Instead we stand up with everyone else and stare intently as Tyson hands Dad the clipboard he's been carrying. Attached is a stack of papers. Probably some sort of contract. Great. Dad hates filling out forms. I hold my breath.

Dad looks the papers up and down, frowns. "What's all this?"

"Just a formality," Tyson explains, "It states that you agree to let us use whatever we record here today."

"And," Billy adds, "that you won't sue *Ghosters* for damaging anything we break by accident if we've used reasonable care."

Tyson raises one finger. "Regardless, if something *does* get broken, we promise to repair or replace it."

Billy nods. "Oh, and also that you'll only be awarded the prize money if we decide the evidence we record here is better than those submitted by the other two finalists." His gaze flicks to Kerry and me, then back to Dad. "That's fair, don't you think?"

After a quick scan, Dad blows his cheeks out, scribbles his name at the bottom, and looks up at Tyson. "Okay, as long as you stick to the areas where the girls have had paranormal experiences, I guess you can all start doing whatever you—"

"Terrific." Tyson shakes Dad's hand and shoots me a wink as Billy heads outside to get things going.

Everyone follows Billy out onto the porch. With a half-dozen neighbors gawking, we watch too as the Junior Ghosters drag their equipment from the vans. Erin carries her computer towers into the house one at a time. A blue plastic cover protects them from the rain. The others haul up some plastic cases, spools of wire, even a folding table and chairs. Once they've gotten everything inside, Tyson claps his hands. "Okay, there's a lot to do before midnight."

CHAPTER 28

IMMEDIATELY, THE JUNIOR Ghosters spring into action. Erin picks up a computer tower, and Kerry dashes down the stairs toward her.

"Need any help?" she asks.

"No thanks, kid. I've got it." Erin slides past Kerry and into the living room, pink hair bouncing.

The other two junior members, a skinny guy with a ponytail and a chunky bald guy, throw open what look like hard, plastic suitcases. By the time it's a quarter to twelve, the Junior Ghosters are almost ready to start. A command center, the folding table, now stands in the middle of the living room where the coffee table used to be. On top, Erin has placed the two computers, some walkie-talkies, and a half-dozen other gadgets that I remember from the show. Cables snake along the floor and Joey helps Erin by sticking duct tape over them so nobody trips.

The ponytail guy hoists his camera up on one shoulder, and the bald guy crouches beside him, fiddling with a second camera at his feet. He glances over at us.

"You girls might want to check your hair," the bald guy suggests. "You *are* going to be on national television."

Oh, god. My hair. I was so worried about Dad letting the Ghosters in, I forgot they'd be interviewing us for the show. Kerry and I bolt for the stairs. If my hair's anything like Kerry's, we both could use a good brushing.

"You did it," Kerry says as we race side by side up the main staircase."

"We're not finished yet," I tell her. "We got the Ghosters inside the house. Now, let's see if the ghosts are as happy about that as we are."

We quickly brush our hair and rush back down.

Billy Joe calls us into the foyer for last minute instructions. "You two know how we do this, right?"

I nod. "Yeah, we watch the show every week."

"Okay, so, we stand here in front of the stairs, I introduce you, and then I ask you to take us around the house to tell us about all your paranormal experiences. Got it?"

What's not to get? We're going to be on TV. We stare at Billy, then at each other. That's when the giggles come. They burst out of us like popcorn in a microwave.

"Hey, serious up." Billy chuckles. "You don't want to go on national TV looking like a couple of goofy school girls, do you?"

"No . . . we don't." I bite my lip to get rid of the permanent grin that's been attached to my face since Dad let them through the front door.

"We'll behave properly," Kerry tells him, obviously struggling to keep her face straight.

Billy peers at each of us through narrowed eyes. "Okay. We're going to start our introductions at the bottom of the main staircase." He leads the way. Tyson and Billy Joe stand on opposite sides of the group with Kerry and me between them. The cameramen are set up over by the front door, cameras perched on their shoulders like big silver vultures.

"Just look into the camera with the red light," Billy tells us.

"What about Joey?" I ask.

His forehead crinkles. "Joey?"

"My brother. He was with us when we filmed the ghost."

Billy shrugs. "Sure, why not."

I peer over at the command station. Joey has already staked out a folding chair alongside Erin, and he's parked in front of one of the computers, chin on his hands.

"Joey," I holler. "Don't you want to be on TV?"

"No, thank you," he says. "I'd rather watch you guys from here."

I look at Billy and shrug.

"Action," the ponytailed cameraman shouts. He holds up three fingers, then two, then one . . .

"Hello, and welcome to a special Halloween edition of *Ghosters*. I'm Tyson O'Seanesey and that guy over there is Billy Joe Francisco. Tonight we're at the home of Theresa Martinez. Together with her friend Kerry Sullivan, these young ladies are finalists in our Third Annual *Ghosters* Video Contest."

Both Kerry and I do a great job of speaking and neither of us gets the giggles. Tyson asks me to show them the parts of the house where I've had paranormal experiences. Since I'm not really sure whether to blame the closed drapes in the dining room on ghosts or Joey's memory, I decide not to mention it.

Kerry and I escort Tyson and Billy Joe into the kitchen where they ask me to go into more detail about the brownie mix. Then we all march down to the basement. I show them where we found the key and explain what happened with the tricycle. After that, we go up to Grandma Carmen's room where I do my best to describe what I saw inside the wardrobe.

Finally, it's time to head up to the third floor. I could tell them about the time I felt something touch my ankle when I accidentally locked myself in there, but I'm in enough trouble with Dad as it is. This is the first time he's heard anything about what happened in the basement and my grandma's room. Throughout the interview, I've sneaked peeks at him, and every time his face has shown a different expression, shock, anger, and what surprises me most, fear.

Tyson continues speaking to the camera as he steps out of my grandmother's bedroom and over to the door to the third floor, just a few strides away. He points at Dad's new addition. "As you can see, a large combination lock has been attached to this door. That's because this door leads up to the third floor, the location where both Theresa and Kerry recorded one of the most amazing apparitions we've ever seen. How remarkable are their recordings?" He prompts the ponytail guy to zoom in on the lock. "Well, right after Theresa's father saw them, he immediately secured the door with this."

What a joke. That's not why Dad put that lock there. He's never seen those recordings. I think about the little ghost and the room it wanted me to see.

At this point, Tyson calls Dad forward and Billy introduces him to the audience. "Mike, would you be so kind as to remove the lock for us?"

Billy motions him toward the door.

With a nervous smile to the camera, Dad shuffles over. After a few spins, the thing drops open.

"Thanks, Mike." Billy Joe moves to open the door, but Dad stays put, smiling into the camera until the bald cameraman waves for him to get out of the away.

And Billy was worried about us kids.

With a stiff nod, Dad finally steps aside.

Billy Joe takes his place, and pulls open the door. "Here we go," he says dramatically. "Up to the forbidden third floor."

Billy flips the light switch on the wall outside the door and leads the way up the stairs, followed by Tyson, me, Kerry, the two cameramen, and Dad. It's weird seeing everything so well lit. It all looks so normal. Once the whole group shuffles out onto the large space at the top of the stairs, Tyson asks me to explain what we saw.

"Right over there is where the ghost appeared." I point at the empty space between two closed doors. "It started out about the size of my fist, but then it grew." I notice I'm hugging myself and look at Dad. He's standing against the wall, arms crossed tight across his chest.

"Obviously, you were both very frightened," Tyson says, positioning himself between me and Kerry. He wraps his arms protectively around us. "Kerry, tell us what happened next?"

She looks into the camera. "So, like Theresa said, it was a ball, but it grew. We were recording it, and it formed into a . . . a . . ."

"A torso?" Billy Joe suggests.

Kerry bites her lower lip. "Yes . . . a torso."

Tyson's eyes sparkle as Kerry retells our story. That ghost scared Kerry and me to death, but Tyson looks like he can't wait to see it.

"Theresa, what happened next?" Tyson asks, his mouth hanging open.

I step back toward the stairs. "We were standing right here, filming, and it started to move." My gaze shifts back and forth between the two cameras. "It came right toward us."

Tyson's lips pucker. "Oooh, I'll bet that was scary. And then what happened?"

"It moved over there." I point. "And passed right through that door."

"Whoah!" Tyson winks at Billy, then smiles at one of the cameras. "Scary stuff, huh? Now, let's turn off the lights and see what mischief Billy and I can stir up."

"And cut," the bald cameraman shouts.

"That was perfect, girls." Tyson gives us each a high five. "When we get back to the studio, Erin will edit your parts into the rest of the show. It'll be awesome."

The crew starts back down the stairs and Billy Joe motions for Kerry and me to join them. "Now comes the fun part."

CHAPTER 29

WE STEP BACK into the living room where Joey's still sitting with Erin at the folding table in front of the two computers. They're both wearing headphones, but unlike Joey, Erin has a wire-thin microphone winding down the side of her face.

Again, everyone starts fiddling with their equipment. The two cameramen switch the regular lights for infrared spotlights. Billy Joe and Tyson check the batteries on their gear and pull night-vision goggles from one of the cases stacked behind Erin. Now, with the help of the infrared equipment, they'll all be able to move through the house in complete darkness.

Kerry bends down to whisper in my ear. "Maybe we'll get to wear some of those goggles too."

"Oh, heck yeah. That would be cool."

With all the preparations going on, Kerry and I are left on our own, so I speak out. "What do you want *us* to do?"

Billy Joe interrupts his conversation with the two cameramen and turns to answer, night-vision goggles perched on his head like some evil scientist. "What we need you to do now is to stay here in the living room. You can sit over there with Erin at the command center and watch what's happening on the computer screens."

"Aw!" Kerry's shoulders sag. "I was hoping we could go along with you."

"Me too," I say, trying not to sound too whiny.

"Sorry girls, but you know we never take non-Ghosters on our explorations."

I offer Billy my best puppy eyes. "What if we promise we'll be super quiet?"

Billy shakes his head no and herds us in the direction of the folding table. "Sorry, but ghosts don't like crowds. Stay with Erin and your brother. I promise you'll be able to see everything really well on those two monitors." He turns back to the cameramen. "Like I was saying, we start in the basement and work our way back through the house, leaving the third floor for the end."

Kerry and I stand there like dummies until Dad waves us over to the three empty chairs that have been set up behind Erin.

"You invited them here," he mutters. "Do what they say."

He's right. I should shut up, be satisfied that the Ghosters are finally here. Still, it would be fun to tag along.

Once the crew disappears into the kitchen, Erin turns off the remaining lights, leaving the house completely dark other than the soft glow of the computer screens. Kerry pulls up a chair next to Erin, and I scooch in between Erin and Joey. Outside, rain batters the covered porch.

Erin glances at my dad. "Mister Martinez, I have one more chair. Don't you want to watch the monitors?"

He shakes his head and sits down on the sofa a few feet behind us. "Looks a little crowded. I'll just sit back here and listen. I'll be close enough . . . *if* there's something to see."

We drag our chairs up closer to the table, and Erin hands us each a pair of headphones, Dad included.

"Why two computers?" Kerry asks.

"Since there are two cameramen," Joey jumps in before Erin can answer, "she needs a monitor to watch what each of them is filming."

I give Erin a crooked smile. "Guess Joey asked you lots of questions, huh?"

She nods, gaze bouncing from one screen to another. "You could say that."

The monitors are large and the pictures are super sharp. Black and white like the full-spectrum camera I'd used to record the ghost. I stare at the screen, amazed. It's really happening. The entire crew of Ghosters is actually here in my house, shuffling down the stairs on their way to explore our basement.

Through the headphones, I hear Billy Joe's voice as he calls into the darkness. "We're looking for Teresa's Grandma Carmen. Is she here?" On one of the screens, he and Tyson pace around, looking a bit silly with their night-vision goggles. Once they get to Grandpa Joe's workshop, they notice the pink tricycle lying on its side in the corner where I'd pushed it. The camera guys film the creepy little thing from every angle.

"Does anyone hear me?" Tyson calls. "Please make a sound. Knock if you can."

Nothing happens. They check out the rest of the basement: the laundry area, the freezer, even the place where we found the dead raccoon.

"I'm picking up a reading on the EMF," Billy announces in a loud whisper. After a minute or so, he locates a metal box attached to the wall and frowns into the camera. "It's only the fuse box."

I look at Kerry and sigh. To my surprise, the Ghosters don't leave. In fact they stay down there a half hour more before giving up.

"I'm surprised they spent so much time down there," Joey says.

Erin, chuckles as we watch the Ghosters team trudge up the stairs. "That's what everybody says. The show's an hour long, but most of our explorations take four or five hours. I edit out the boring stuff back at the office."

Once the Ghosters get to the kitchen, they peek into the pantry and poke around in the cupboards. As far as I know, the only thing that ever happened there was the business with the brownie mix. Still, they spend twenty minutes trying to get a ghost to turn on a flashlight before coming back to the main staircase.

Tyson peeks into the living room before starting up the stairs. "Don't worry, girls. We still have lots more house to see."

Their next stop is Grandma Carmen's room. Billy opens the wardrobe. When nothing happens, they decide to get aggressive.

"You know what?" Billy says in a loud voice. "I'm tired. I think I'm going to lie down on this bed for a while." He stretches out on the bed, hands clasped behind his head.

"Me too," Tyson says, and without warning he takes a running leap and lands hard enough on the bed that Billy grabs hold of the headboard to not bounce off.

Joey gasps. "He's lucky he didn't break it."

"If that ghost really is your grandma, that *had* to tick her off," Kerry says.

I smile, thinking of what my own mom would have done if she'd caught me doing that.

Tyson and Billy lie sprawled on the bed, all the while calling to any ghost who might be up for a chat. Nothing happens, and one of the cameramen passes Billy something black, about the size and shape of a coffee mug. He turns it on and the thing starts to hiss and crackle, the kind of noise you hear when switching from one radio station to the next.

Billy shows it to the camera. "This is called a Spirit Box."

We can barely hear him over the noise.

Joey yanks his headphones off and rubs his ears.

Back in Grandma Carmen's room, Billy continues with his explanation. "A Spirit Box uses FM radio frequency sweeps to generate white noise," he says, raising his voice to be heard over the static. "Theories suggest that these boxes give spirits energy so we can hear them speak."

"Carmen Ramos, are you here?" Tyson says, practically shouting. "Come out and talk to us."

"Yeah." Billy Joe laughs. "Come in here and push Tyson off the bed. That was very disrespectful of him jumping onto it like that. Come and teach him a lesson."

Again nothing happens, and Billy gets up and squirts some of Grandma Carmen's perfume around the room. "Mrs. Ramos, you have excellent taste. If you don't want me wasting your perfume, do something. Show us you're here."

After that, the static cuts off for just a second, and we hear a murmuring sound. For a moment, everybody gets excited. It might be a woman, but it's garbled, and nobody can make out the words. After that, no matter how much the Ghosters beg, nothing comes of it.

Was that Grandma Carmen? Why the heck didn't she talk to them? I scowl at Kerry, and she scowls back just as hard.

The next room the crew enters is right next to Grandma Carmen's. It's a sewing room. My mom sewed a little too, but Grandma Carmen had tons more sewing equipment than she did. Cameras scan shelves crowded with plastic containers. There are also quite a few stacks of cardboard boxes, making it tough for the men to move around. Monitor one shows that the bald cameraman is standing back, while on monitor two, the ponytail guy weaves in and around the stacks.

"Whoa!" Ponytail shouts. His camera image bounces as he leaps back, surprising everyone.

Holy crabs! Was that a headless woman?

"What was that?" Kerry shouts.

My gaze leaps from one monitor to the other.

Upstairs, the crew bursts out laughing. The view from Ponytail's camera suddenly does a nosedive. We see shoes, a flash of the wall. It settles down, and we discover that Tyson has his arms wrapped around someone. I hold my breath as he wrestles her out of the corner.

"Just a dress form," he announces.

The bald guy's camera shows us a grinning Ponytail, his chest still heaving from the shock.

I lean back in my chair, heart pounding.

"It's like a mannequin," Tyson explains as he poses with the half-dressed headless figure. "Seamstresses use them for fitting clothes."

Once they're all tired of teasing Ponytail, Tyson tries the Spirit Box again. Nobody answers their questions, so they try the other rooms. Sadly, the ghosts aren't feeling chatty.

After another hour of disappointment and frustration, the group heads toward the door to the third floor.

"Looks like a bust," Tyson mumbles.

I reach behind Erin's chair and give Kerry's hand a squeeze.

She squeezes back. "It's not over yet."

CHAPTER 30

AS THE GHOSTERS shuffle through the doorway, Tyson starts his narration again. "We're heading up to the third floor now. It was at the top of these very stairs that Theresa and Kerry took the amazing footage that got them into this competition." He backs up the stairs, talking to Ponytail's camera the whole way. "At first their apparition was a sort of cloudy ball, but it soon developed into a full torso with a head and two arms." He reaches the top of the staircase. "And it all happened . . . right . . . here."

The Ghosters try everything they've got: the spirit box, the flashlight trick we were going to use in Grandma's wardrobe, as well as some new doodads I've never seen before. None of their equipment shows the least bit of activity.

"This sucks," Kerry groans. "Our recordings were real. What's the matter with that ghost, anyway?"

"Heck if I know." I look from one computer monitor to the other. What if it's too scared to show itself?

At the sight of Tyson and Billy wandering around the third floor, I remember the lies Dad told us about how damaged the floors were. Ever since he caught us up there, I've been afraid to ask about it. Now, the Ghosters have given me a burst of courage. I turn, barely able to see him even though he's just a few feet away on the sofa.

"Hey Dad," I call out. "Why did you tell us the third floor was dangerous? It looks fine."

He shrugs and stares up at the ceiling. "All I know is what your grandfather told me."

Dad's answer sounds rehearsed. I remember the night I'd spied on him from the darkness of the back stairs. Maybe I should challenge him, tell him how I'd seen him rub his hand on that door as if some lost love was trapped behind it. But I can't. It's the wrong time *and* the wrong place. With my little blast of bravery all fizzled out, I turn back to the computer monitors.

Tyson is standing beside the claw foot table and turning in slow circles. "Okay. There are four doors. Let's see what's behind them."

To my shock, Dad suddenly tears his headphones off and dashes around to the other side of the folding table. There's a walkie-talkie next to Erin. He snatches it.

"Tyson, do you hear me?"

"Yes, Mike, I hear you. Is there a problem?"

Dad steps off into the shadows on the other side of the room, but I can still make out the conversation. "I thought you were just going to explore the places where the girls experienced something. You never said anything about going into the other rooms."

"That's true, Mike. We didn't *plan* on entering those rooms, but since we haven't gotten any activity so far, we figured we might as well check out the rest of the place. You want to win the contest, don't you?"

"I'd really rather you didn't go in there," Dad says in a lowered voice.

Does this have to do with why he yanked me back from that door before I could open it? "Why can't they look?" I ask from across the room. "The floors are safe."

Dad pulls the radio away from his face. "Please, Theresa, stay out of this."

But I'm not staying out of it. I stride across the room, and he moves away from me as he continues his conversation.

"Tyson, I don't want the crew going into any more rooms, do you understand? Make them come back downstairs."

But Tyson won't give in. "Mike, if you'd read the contract more carefully, you would know that you've given us permission to access every part of this house. So, after driving half way across the country, we're going to check out those other rooms."

"Tyson . . . please." Dad's voice is strained. "You can try going down to the basement again."

"Sorry. Been there, done that."

Even in the darkness, Dad sounds desperate. He's been hiding something, and now it's about to come out. Is that what I really want? Feeling more than a little guilty, I watch as he glares at the radio, then over at me as if he's trying to decide on something.

"Fine. Do what you want!" he barks into the radio.

I flinch. Yelling at people he barely knows is not Dad's thing. Maybe I've pushed him too far.

I take a step back as he comes at me. To my surprise, he's not angry anymore. It's like shouting at Tyson has drained all the fight out of him. He looks down at me, his eyes dark hollows in the gloomy light.

"I should have known you'd eventually find out," he tells me. "Why couldn't you just do what I said and stay away from there?"

"But, Dad, I did this for you. I thought you'd be proud of me if we—"

"Proud? Of you going behind my back, of tricking those people into coming here?" He rests his hand on my shoulder. "Be careful what you wish for, Theresa."

Not sure what to do, I stand there, lip quivering. What have I gotten myself into? Weighed down by guilt and confusion, I follow him back to the command center.

The monitors show the Ghosters have already stepped into one of the rooms. There's nothing there, just old curtains and dusty hardwood floors. The next room is pretty much the same. The third is a storage closet. Antique vacuum cleaner, old lamps, boxes. Again, no ghosts. Nothing to earn us that prize money. Nothing that would explain Dad's weird behavior. But what about the room the ghost wanted me to see? Always looking for drama, the Ghosters have left that one for last.

Tyson steps over to the door and wraps his fingers around the knob. "Okay, folks, this is it, the last door. The one Theresa and Kerry watched the little ghost pass through. The door the spirit wanted Theresa to open." He stares, straight-faced, into the camera. "And we have no idea what's behind it."

Well, somebody knows what's behind it. I look up at Dad, who's standing behind Joey. He looks tired. Heartbroken. I've seen that look before. At my mother's funeral.

CHAPTER 31

THE DOOR OPENS onto a hallway lined on both sides by identical closets, drawers, and shelves filling both walls from floor to ceiling. I don't know what I was expecting, but it wasn't this.

I drag my chair even closer to Erin's computer screens.

A few spiders have set up housekeeping in this hallway too, and Billy and Tyson get busy knocking down webs before leading the crew through. The cameramen pan all around, making sure to show each of the little toys and books that sit on the shelves, abandoned in the gloom.

"These toys must have belonged to a small child, obviously a little girl," Tyson says.

Billy Joe picks up a toy tiara from a shelf and brushes away the cobwebs. "From the looks of things, they've probably been here a few years."

The cameras miss nothing as they follow the Ghosters down the corridor. One focuses on a tiny plastic tea set and something clicks in my memory. A tea party. Another little girl. Wide-eyed, I look to my father. It's too dark to be sure, but I think there's a tear trickling down his cheek. Should say something? But what?

My eyes ping pong from one monitor to the other as Tyson and Billy step out of the hallway and into a room. Tyson stands in the center, turning a slow circle. "This seems to be a playroom."

I jab a finger at one of the screens and squint up at Dad, still standing behind Joey. "Was that *Mom's* playroom when she was little? Why didn't you show me before?"

He opens his mouth, chin trembling. "Theresa—"

"Look." Joey points. "Two toy kitchens, two paint easels . . ."

Like everything else in the room, the easels are tiny. There are finger paintings still clipped to them, and the childish abstracts are cracked and flaking. So, if this was my mom's room, why did she have two of everything? She was an only child . . . wasn't she?

Billy Joe crosses the dusty hardwood floor and disappears through a doorway on the far wall. After a few seconds, he's back. "I found another room with two cribs."

I look at the others. "Did he just say there were *two* cribs?"

Kerry shakes her head. "I am totally confused."

She's confused. I feel like my head's going to explode.

"Let's have a closer look at these." Tyson heads for a pair of wooden rocking horses sitting in front of a wide curtained window. He motions for one of the cameramen to follow him over.

Whose room is this? It's like I'd been putting together a jigsaw puzzle and someone all of a sudden switched the pieces on me.

I leap to my feet. "Okay, this is nuts. Unless Mom had a sister I don't know about, this makes absolutely no sense."

Tyson leans down, hands on knees. "Looking closer, I see that each of the rocking horses has a name stamped onto the saddle." He kneels beside the closest. "This one says Isabel."

Isabel? So Mom had a sister named—

He turns to the other. "And this one says Theresa."

"Theresa?" I gasp. Then who's Isabel? And why would she have all the same stuff as me?" All of a sudden, images of two small girls on red and pink tricycles flash through my mind.

"Oh my God. Did I have a twin sister?" My legs give out and I stumble back.

Dad grabs me and helps me back into my chair. I want to scream questions at him, force him to explain. But the Ghosters are still upstairs, and they're excited about something.

Both monitors show Billy grinning and holding the EMF meter up to the camera. "Look, we're finally getting some readings. They're strong, too. See? Five lights."

"Check to see if it's caused by something electrical," Tyson says as he gets back to his feet.

Billy circles the room, but finds nothing to explain even a weak electromagnetic field.

"Look." He points at his arm and the camera zooms in. "The hairs are sticking up."

"The temperature is dropping fast," Tyson says.

He holds a thermometer for the Ponytail guy to zoom in on. Something off screen catches his attention.

"Will you look at that . . ." His voice is barely a whisper as he stares across the room through his night-vision goggles. Both cameras swing in that direction.

Something is forming over one of the rocking horses, like dust and light blending together. When it's done, a small girl, no more than two years old, sits on the leather saddle. Not smoke, but not solid either. The toddler leans forward and grabs the handles with her chubby hands, and the wooden horse creaks as it begins to rock.

"This is amazing," Billy whispers. "It's like she's made of—"

"—liquid glass," Tyson finishes.

I think back to the little ghost we recorded, the picture Kerry found in the shoebox from Grandma Carmen's wardrobe. How stupid I've been. That little girl riding the pink tricycle . . . it wasn't even me. Tears stream down my cheeks, but I keep my eyes on the screen.

"That's Isabel, isn't it, Daddy? That's my sister. How could you and Mom not tell me about her?"

"We thought it was for the best," he mumbles, voice cracking. "It was . . . complicated."

I wipe my tears away and turn to Erin. "Do you have any more infrared goggles?"

"I think so." Erin turns in her chair and points at the

equipment boxes stacked against the wall. "They're in there, somewhere."

I open the top one, shove the empty plastic case aside, and throw open the next. "I found some."

Joey runs over. "I want to go too. Is there a pair for me?"

"Sorry, Jojo, these are the last ones." I strap on the goggles and turn them on as I'd seen Tyson do earlier.

Kerry tries to pass Joey a flashlight, but Erin grabs her arm. "No. No flashlights."

Joey nods, but I see the disappointment in his face.

I squeeze his hand and run off into the darkness.

"Be careful with those goggles!" Erin shouts after me.

CHAPTER 32

I GET TO the nursery, and the spirit of my newly discovered sister is still there, rocking away on her little wooden horse with the entire *Ghosters* crew watching. Is she waiting for *me*? I pull off the goggles and allow my eyes to adjust to the dark before tiptoeing into the room. Tyson was right. If Isabel wasn't moving, you'd think she was sculpted out of glass. A soft shimmer radiates from her, and although she's far from human, I feel a connection.

The name sticks in my throat, but I push it out in a trembling whisper, "Isabel?"

My little ghost-sister stops rocking and looks up at me. *Teesa.*

I hear it, even though her lips don't move.

Leaning forward, she holds out a tiny hand. She wants me to come closer.

The Ghosters move aside and I shuffle past them, heart beating through my chest. I kneel beside her, and she smiles.

Tears spill down my face. I wonder what Joey thinks. Dad too, for that matter. "I don't understand. What happened . . . ?"

Isabel's lips part. "*It not you fault, Teesa. Talk to Daddy,*" she says in a soft baby voice.

Not my fault? What, my sister's death? As I sit on my heels, puzzling over Isabel's words, love radiates from her, warming me. I wish Joey were here to feel it. Boy, would *he* have questions.

Sensing that we don't have much time, I slide myself forward. Can you touch a ghost? Let's find out. I reach out my hand.

"*Teesa* . . ." Her voice is high and sweet and her giggle makes me chuckle. It's just like the one Kerry and I recorded back in Grandma Carmen's room. She raises her hand, tiny and shimmering. Just as it seems we'll touch, a burst of emotion surges through me. It's love, painless, but I gasp all the same. A moment later there's a dazzling flash of light and my sister is gone.

For a moment, nobody moves. Then Billy steps to the door and turns on the ceiling light, eyes wide with wonder. "I saw it and I still can't believe it."

Tyson steps in front of the cameras. "Tell me you guys got that."

"I had to change the battery twice," the bald guy says, looking at his camera screen, "but yeah. I got it."

Like me, the ponytailed guy had been kneeling, and Tyson pulls him to his feet. "How about you? Did you capture the voice?"

He plays some back and grins. "All of it." He sets his camera on the floor and high fives everyone.

"This has to be the best paranormal event ever recorded!" Billy Joe shouts. "Theresa, there's no doubt about it . . . you won the . . ."

I run past him, headed for the living room. Dad has some explaining to do.

CHAPTER 33

A RED-EYED DAD meets me at the bottom of the stairs. He grips my shoulders and promises to tell me everything once the *Ghosters* have said their goodbyes. Billy Joe and Tyson want Isabel's story too, but Dad's not sharing. The vans pull out of our driveway just as the grandfather clock chimes three times. It's great that we won the contest, but right now I'm more interested in learning about my sister.

Dad herds the three of us into the living room. Kerry and Joey sit on the sofa. I drop between them, body exhausted, mind whirling. Joey yawns. Dad heads for the stairs.

"Where are you going?" I call after him.

"To your grandmother's sewing room. There's something there you need to see."

Kerry squeezes my hand. "Your brain must be scrambled about now."

"You got that right. I had a twin sister, and they didn't even tell me."

Joey bumps my leg with his. "If it makes you feel any better, they didn't tell me either."

That's right. Isabel was his sister too.

I bump him back and nod, remembering the day I overheard Dad's phone call with Tita Gloria. He was talking about a risk and not having any choice about something. At the time I thought he was stressing over the move and upsetting Joey with all the changes. But now, I'm not so sure. Dad's been acting weird ever since we moved in, and now I know why. No wonder he didn't want us snooping around the third floor.

The three of us look toward the staircase, waiting for Dad to come back.

After a few minutes, he does. He's carrying what looks like an overstuffed binder.

"Would you mind if I switch places with you?" he asks Kerry.

"No problem." Her gaze flashes from the binder back to me as she hops up and moves behind the sofa to peer over our shoulders.

Dad squeezes in between me and Joey and rests the fat binder on his lap. "Isabel was right. It *is* time you know."

I stare as he pats the book with his hand. Poor guy, he looks like he's aged five years since dinner.

The first pictures are of the day we were born. There we lie, Isabel and Theresa, side by side, and as far as I can tell, identical. There's one of Mom in her hospital bed, smiling, holding a baby in each arm. There are more of us as we leave the hospital, at home, being bathed, fed. Lots more with us sleeping, our arms wrapped around each other. The pictures show us taking our first steps and eating cake on our first and second birthdays. In others we're gathering Easter eggs, fighting over Christmas presents, and even riding the pink and red tricycles around the big patio in Grandma Carmen's backyard.

"You know it's funny." I reach across and close the binder. "I've always had a feeling something was missing from my life. Why didn't you tell me about her?"

Tears rim Dad's eyes. "First of all, I want you to understand that your mother and I didn't make this decision easily. We worried that if you knew the truth . . ."

If I knew what? A knot grows in my chest. "Tell me, Dad. Tell me what happened to my sister."

For the first time since forever, Dad takes my hand. "Haven't you ever wondered why your mom never visited or spoke to your grandmother for all of those years?"

I shrug. "Mom said they had some sort of fight when I was little."

"That's true, but before you . . ." He takes a deep breath

and blows it out as he pushes a loose strand of hair from my face. "Before *that*, you two stayed with your grandparents quite a bit. They loved taking care of you, and your grandfather made you that amazing nursery upstairs. He also built you those two rocking horses."

I nod and sniffle, waiting for him to continue.

"So one day your mom and I left you with your grandparents while we went to Lake Tahoe for the weekend. Your grandmother took you and Isabel out in the backyard." He sighs again and smiles sadly. "You girls sure loved riding your tricycles around that swimming pool."

Tears flow down my face as I imagine what happened next.

"From what Carmen told us, she was out there reading a magazine while you and Isabel were sitting in the grass playing with your toys. One of your grandmother's friends was having surgery that day and the husband had promised to call afterward. When the phone rang, Carmen didn't want to miss the call, so she went inside." His forehead creases as he recalls the painful day. "She was only gone a couple of minutes, but that's all it took. When she got back, Isabel was at the bottom of the pool, along with your red tricycle."

I squeeze his hand. "So, that's why Mom wouldn't talk to Grandma. She blamed her for Isabel drowning."

"Yes." His gaze meets mine. "We both did. But we also thought you might have pushed your sister in."

"Why would I push my own sister into the pool?" I gasp. No wonder he's always favored Joey. And I thought it was because of the Asperger's.

"You see, when you were little, you loved each other to death," his voice cracks, "but you also fought like cats and dogs over anything you could get your hands on."

"Is that why the nursery has two of everything?" I ask, chest pounding.

He stares across the room at the blank TV screen, eyes moist with tears. "You were our first kids. We should have taught you how to share, but having twins was wearing on us. Instead, we decided to take the easy way out. Identical dolls . . . two paint easels. That worked out fine with most of your toys . . ."

"But not the tricycles." Joey's voice surprises me. All this time he's been sitting there, not saying a word. Kerry too. I almost forgot they were there.

Kerry comes around the sofa and drops onto Dad's recliner. "It all makes sense now. That's why Theresa remembered having a red tricycle. There were two . . . a red one *and* a pink one."

Dad nods and wipes his cheek with the heel of his hand. The more I hear, the more everything falls into place.

"When your grandmother came back outside, you were alone, lying on the edge of the pool with your arm in the water, wet to the elbow. You were crying, and all you could say was, 'Isa bad' and 'No, no. My trike.' Isabel was at the bottom of the pool, and since your red tricycle was down there too, your grandmother assumed you and Isabel had been fighting over it."

"It was all your grandmother's fault. Your mom couldn't forgive her for leaving you two out there by yourselves. We never blamed you, Theresa. But we did worry that if you grew up knowing what happened you might hold yourself responsible someday. I'm sorry for all the secrets, honey, but we just didn't want to take that chance. It could have ruined your life."

"Maybe you did blame me," I mumble.

"What? No. Why would you say that?"

"You've always treated Joey nicer than me."

"No, I . . ." he looks at Joey. "Son, is Theresa right? Have I been nicer to you than her?"

"I'm not sure what she means by nicer. Mom hugged Theresa all the time. She said nice words and smiled at her." For the first time ever, Joey's holding Dad's gaze. "You smile at me a lot too, but you barely look at Theresa."

Dad shakes his head like he can't believe it.

"Joey's right," I sob. "I told myself it was because he needs you more since he's got . . ." I look at Joey, then Dad, unsure how to go on.

"My Asperger's." Joey leans across and surprises me by patting my hand. "That's okay, Theresa. It's not a secret."

Mouth open, Dad looks from me to Joey, then back again. "No . . . I wouldn't."

The words spill out of me. "Maybe you blame me for Mom too."

Dad leaps to his feet as if he's been shocked by a thousand volts. "No . . . no . . . !" He takes my hand and pulls me to my feet. "Is that really what you think? That I blame you for your mother's death?"

I blink up at him through the tears. "Well . . . ?"

"Honey, no. Teenagers ran that red light, not you. If I've been paying more attention to Joey, it's because of the Asperger's, not—"

"When's the last time you hugged me, Daddy?"

For a while he just stares, tears trickling down his cheeks. Then, as if a light has clicked on in his head, he pulls me close and hugs me to his chest.

"My god, Theresa. I've been so angry since your mother's death, and you're so much like her . . . strong, competent." He takes my face in his hands. "I guess I got so caught up in my own misery that I didn't realize you were suffering too, what with all the changes you've had to deal with, moving . . . starting a new school. And you never complained. You even volunteered to do the cooking. I'm not mad at you. I'm proud, and I apologize for not telling you sooner."

The more I hear him talk the angrier I get. I pull back. "That's it? Sorry? You and Mom lied to me. You should have told me about Isabel. I lost my sister *and* my grandparents that day. And now I'm supposed to forgive you just because you hug me? Maybe I did push Isabel into the water, but whose fault is that anyway?" I stand up. "Maybe if you guys weren't always dumping us with our grandparents I'd still have a sister."

"Theresa, wait. You're not being fair." Kerry tries to stop me but I push her hand aside and head for the kitchen where I slam the back door behind me and run out into the yard.

It's not raining anymore, but at this hour it's cold. Windy too, but there's no way I'm going back inside for a sweater. The motion lights Dad installed last week flash on as I march across the weed-choked grass to the pool. Shivering, I sit on the edge, hugging myself. My hair whips my face as leaves cartwheel through the shadows. Dad cleaned most of the gunk from the deep end, but there's still no water. Considering what I've just learned, it makes sense he's in no rush to get it filled.

I shouldn't have said that to him, but, my God, all these years and they never even mention her? Even Tita Gloria was in on it. It's like they all wanted to wipe Isabel from existence.

I stare up at the sky, still scattered with clouds. But my sister did exist. For two-and-a-half years we ate, slept, and played together, until . . .

There's a gust of wind, and across the pool the busted straps of Grandma Carmen's chaise longue flap and sway. I turn and peer up at the house. Even now, its windows are still lit from top to bottom. Papa Joe lived for three years after Isabel died and Grandma Carmen, for eight. I wonder if Isabel ever appeared to them.

After a while, the motion lights click off, and the pool goes black. It's like I'm sitting on the side of a cliff.

You know, toddlers are notoriously bad at sharing.

Startled, I turn back to find Mom sitting on the edge of the pool beside me, still dressed in the same white capris and tee-shirt from my dream. If not for the fuzzy edges and her hair not moving from the wind, she looks almost real.

"Mom . . . you . . . you're . . ." It's just like the dream.

A ghost, yes. She stares into the empty pool, smiling

sadly. *I'm really sorry things worked out this way, Theresa. You're angry, but try not to resent your dad for too long. Like he said, we kept Isabel's death a secret because we thought it would be best for you in the long run.*

Strangely, our conversation feels so normal that I'm not scared. But I'm still fuming, so I cross my arms, determined to stay that way. "It's not just Dad I'm mad at. It's you too."

I know.

"*And* Grandma. She should have known better than to—"

Leave you babies out there alone?

The female voice comes from behind. I look over my shoulder. Grandma Carmen is standing there wearing the same dress she had on when she took the picture that's sitting on the living room mantle. Like Mom, the wind doesn't seem to touch her.

Chin lowered, my ghostly grandmother shakes her head slowly. *It was a horrible mistake, Theresa, and something I had to live with for the rest of my life.*

I scramble to my feet, staring wide-eyed at my grandmother's ghost.

Mom stands too and rests her hand on my shoulder. It feels cool. Tingly.

Your sister's death had a terrible effect on all of our lives, she tells me. *Like you, I felt my mother had let me down. I was furious.*

We never spoke again, Grandma says.

That's eight years, Mom reminds me. *Eight years neither of us would ever get back. You don't want that to happen with your father, do you?*

"No, I . . ." Tears burst from me. "I'm just sick of all the dishonesty. I want it all out."

With a grim twist of the mouth, Grandma points down at the edge of the pool where I was sitting just a few moments earlier. *Sit.*

A little surprised, I look at Mom. She nods. I drop down and hang my legs over the side again.

Close your eyes, Grandma says.

So I do. For a moment, nothing happens. But soon the wind stops. My skin starts to warm, and the inside of my eyelids go red, like when you close your eyes and turn your face up to the sun.

You can open your eyes now.

There we are, Little Theresa and Little Isabel, sitting on a blanket, surrounded by newly mown grass and freshly clipped shrubs. A few feet away, Grandma Carmen suns herself on a chaise longue with an open magazine draped across her chest. And me? I'm still sitting right where I am, but now there's water halfway up my calves and the sun's beating down on me.

Not knowing what else to do, I stir the water with my feet and wait. After a few moments, the phone rings inside. Grandma gets up. She tells us to stay right where we are, that she'll be back in a minute. If the girls would just continue to play with their toys, everything would be fine. But no.

For whatever reason, Theresa decides it's the perfect time to ride her tricycle. She starts pedaling around the pool. Safe enough, but then Isabel climbs on her trike too and she's pedaling in the opposite direction. When they meet on the far side of the pool, the sidewalk is too narrow for them to pass. Isabel is furious. If it were any other place in the yard, she could get around me by pulling her tricycle out onto the grass, but there, a thick hedge blocks her way.

"Teesa, go." She bumps her front wheel into mine again and again.

"No!" my baby-self bellows. My feet rock on the pedals as I try to move forward.

Howling in frustration, Isabel climbs off her pink tricycle. I climb off mine and we continue to bang them into each other. Since that doesn't get us anywhere, Isabel decides she wants my red trike instead. She pushes my hands off the handlebars and tries to take it from me.

"No!" I shout. "Bad Isa! My trike!"

She slaps me away. I plop down on the sidewalk crying as Isabel struggles with turning my tricycle around. Back and forth, Isabel jerks the handlebars and stamps her feet when the front tire gets twisted around backward. With one especially hard thrust she loses her balance and stumbles.

In the blink of an eye, I'm not watching from across the pool anymore. I'm right there, thrusting out my hand, my two-year-old hand, reaching for my falling sister. But I guess toddlers aren't known for their lightning-fast reflexes. Helpless, all I can do is watch as both Isabel and my red tricycle slip over the side and into the water. Crying, I kneel at the edge of the pool, stare through the ripples as my sister sinks to the bottom. Grandma is gone for only a few minutes, but that's more than enough. When she returns, I'm still reaching into the water for Isabel. Grandma screams.

I look up and point at the water, shouting, "Bad Isa! My trike!"

You can open your eyes now.

A deep moan flows out of me and I fall back on my elbows breathing hard. Mom and Grandma are standing on either side of me, or should I say hovering since their feet barely graze the concrete walkway.

I think about what I just experienced and sob. Having lived it, it's clear that my baby-self was talking about Isabel taking away her trike. But I can understand why Grandma thought I pushed her into the water.

"I . . . I tried to help her."

Yes, Grandma says. *But I didn't know that. From the way you were talking . . .*

Look, Mom says. *We all agree that leaving you girls out there unsupervised was wrong, but so was the way your dad and I reacted. Your grandmother didn't mean for Isabel to die just like your father didn't mean to hurt you. He loves you, Theresa. You heard him say it. Please, find it in yourself to forgive him. He knows he messed up.* She takes Grandma Carmen's hand. *Don't waste your life resenting him.*

They wait, staring down at me with pleading eyes.

I try to stand but end up on all fours, a little woozy after the experience. "Okay." I wipe my eyes, draw in a deep breath, and push myself to my feet. "You're right . . . I *should* forgive him."

I look down as a small but familiar figure peeks out from between them. It's Isabel.

Mom glances up at the sky, then scoops Isabel up and rests her on her hip. She turns back to me, looking not only relieved, but a little sad too. *I'm so happy you feel that way, baby. But now that everything is as it should be, we have to go. Just remember . . . we love you, and we'll always be watching over you.*

Isabel stretches her hand toward me, so Mom steps closer and my little ghost-twin pats my cheek. Smiling, she gives me a tingly but wet baby kiss and says, *Bye-bye, Teesa. You kiss Daddy too, okay?*

"Sure, I'll kiss Daddy." *How can I hold a grudge when three ghosts tell me not to?*

There's a flash of light, and I find myself sitting back on the side of the pool. Alone.

"Mom . . . ? Grandma . . . ? Isabel . . . ? Were you even here?" I stare up at the sky, now sparkling with stars. Does it matter? Smiling, I jump up and run back into the house.

Diana Corbitt is a retired elementary school teacher who has lived her entire life in northern California. She has two sons who, although grown up and out of the house, still live nearby. Ever since she was a kid she loved to be scared, either by movies or books. She started writing her first story in sixth grade. That one never got past six pages, but now that she's retired she can't stop writing. Her work has appeared in *Bewildering Stories* and *Encounters Magazine*. She had a podcast on Manor House and one of her short stories was published in an anthology entitled *Wax and Wane: A Gathering of Witch Tales*. When she's not trying to scare herself silly, Diana enjoys working with stained glass, travel, and going to the movies. They don't all have to be scary. Just not chick flicks.

CPSIA information can be obtained
at www.ICGtesting.com
Printed in the USA
FSOW01n0432260118
43811FS